Tess kept her eyes closed. She had no idea how or why this miracle had occurred, but she didn't want it to end.

His voice was a whisper. "Tess, I need to—"

"Don't talk."

For five long and desperate years, she'd been alone. She was a widow, a single mom. Those years were a famine. And now, she was hungry. She wanted to touch every part of him—on the inside and on the surface. He was back. Joe had come back to her.

Am I losing my mind? Logically, this could not be. She reached higher until she was holding his face in her hands. Eyes still closed, she kissed him again. *Oh my God, it was him.* She knew. Without the slightest doubt, she knew. He was the love of her life, her soul mate, the father of her son.

CASSIE MILES

BABY BATTALION

TORONTO NEW YORK LONDON
AMSTERDAM PARIS SYDNEY HAMBURG
STOCKHOLM ATHENS TOKYO MILAN MADRID
PRAGUE WARSAW BUDAPEST AUCKLAND

Special thanks and acknowledgment to Cassie Miles for her
contribution to the Daddy Corps series.

Recycling programs
for this product may
not exist in your area.

ISBN-13: 978-0-373-69584-3

BABY BATTALION

www.Harlequin.com

Printed in U.S.A.

ABOUT THE AUTHOR

Though born in Chicago and raised in L.A., Cassie Miles has lived in Colorado long enough to be considered a semi-native. The first home she owned was a log cabin in the mountains overlooking Elk Creek, with a thirty-mile commute to her work at the *Denver Post*.

After raising two daughters and cooking tons of macaroni and cheese for her family, Cassie is trying to be more adventurous in her culinary efforts. Ceviche, anyone? She's discovered that almost anything tastes better with wine. When she's not plotting Harlequin Intrigue books, Cassie likes to hang out at the Denver Botanical Gardens near her high-rise home.

Books by Cassie Miles

CAST OF CHARACTERS

Tess Donovan—A single mom and successful events planner in Washington, D.C., she was widowed five years ago.

Nolan Law—Scarred by battle injuries, he was the first man hired for CSal and usually takes charge.

Joe Donovan—Tess's deceased husband and the love of her life.

Joey Donovan—The 4-year-old son of Tess and Joe, he was born after his father died.

Trudy Bensen—The office manager and assistant for Tess's business.

Bart Bellows—The 75-year-old founder of CSal, who has been kidnapped.

Victor Bellows—Bart's son is supposedly MIA.

Wes Bradley—The alias used by Victor Bellows.

Lila Lockhart—The Governor of Texas hired Tess to plan her event at the Smithsonian.

Stacy Giordano—The governor's aide keeps everything running smoothly.

Zachary Giordano—Stacy's son.

Omar Harris—Nolan's CIA contact.

The Zamir family—Clients who use Tess to plan events.

Pierre LeBrun—The haughty chef is nothing but trouble for Tess in her event planning.

Greenaway—A powerful drug and weapons dealer who has sworn to take violent revenge on Bart Bellows and Joe Donovan.

Chapter One

Five years after her husband's death, Tess Donovan still sometimes imagined that she heard the sound of his laughter in a crowd. Whenever she saw a marine in dress blues, she remembered Joe standing at attention—so handsome with his perfect profile and fine features. If he hadn't been involved in so many secret operations, they could have used his gorgeous face for recruitment posters.

Her cab drove along Constitution Avenue, and she peered through the rear window, trying to see the National Christmas Tree in the Ellipse outside the White House. During the holiday season, she missed Joe like crazy. They had always attended the ceremonial lighting of the tree. They'd shopped together for presents, danced together at dozens of holiday galas. Their Christmases had been all about silver bells and snowball fights and hot buttered rum in front of the fireplace.

That was then. This was now.

She sank back in the seat. Starting with the New Year, she vowed to get on with her life. Not that she'd been standing still for five years. As the single mother of a four-and-a-half-year-old son, she seldom got the chance to sit down, and her small catering business had grown into a successful event-planning enterprise. When it came to mothering and working, she was holding her own. It was her personal life that sucked. In five years, she'd only been on a handful of dates, none of which had turned out well. None of those men were Joe.

This year would be different. She'd give herself the chance to meet a special man. It shouldn't be that hard; she was only thirty-two and not bad looking, with black hair and blue eyes. She deserved a mate. And her son deserved a father.

Exiting her cab outside the National Museum of American History, she heard a group of strolling carolers. The tenor sounded just like Joe; he had loved to belt out a rock-and-roll version of "Santa Claus is Coming to Town."

Dusk came early in December. She glanced over her shoulder toward the towering Washington Monument, already lit and gleaming. Then she saw something that made her look twice. Her eyes were lying. This couldn't be. She looked again.

There he was. Joe was walking toward her. She recognized his square shoulders and long stride. In spite of the chill, his trench coat was unbuttoned. He had never minded the cold.

The rational part of her mind told her that she was wrong. Joe was dead, buried at Arlington. But she couldn't control her imagination. Her heart skipped. Her fingers lost their grip on her briefcase.

She wanted to run to him and throw herself into his arms. He'd lift her off the sidewalk and twirl her in a circle. And they'd be happy again.

As he came closer, she stared—knowing that he wasn't Joe but hoping for a miracle. He was less than ten feet from her. Their gazes locked, and she saw him clearly. His was the face of a stranger—a young man in his early twenties. Joe would have been thirty-eight by now. Clearly, she was losing her mind.

The stranger smiled politely, picked up her briefcase and placed it in her hands. "Merry Christmas," he said.

"Same to you."

Not Joe, he wasn't Joe, of course, he wasn't. Though she felt like melting into a weepy puddle on the sidewalk, Tess pulled herself together. She straightened the lapels on her burgundy wool winter coat, tucked her shoulder-length hair behind her ears and firmly grasped the handle of her briefcase as she ascended the stairs into the museum. With every stride across the marble floors, the heels of her sensible black pumps clicked, and she gathered herself. She couldn't afford to act like a delusional, sentimental mess. This was business.

In less than a week, on Christmas Eve, Tess was responsible for a sit-down dinner for three hundred in the second floor Flag Hall. The sponsor of this event—Governor Lila Lockhart of Texas—was celebrating the donation of several artifacts to the Smithsonian as well as thanking some of the top donors to Texans in Congress. Tess had never handled such a prestigious event, and she wanted to get every detail right.

In the waiting area outside the office of the Special Events Coordinator, she greeted the governor's aide, Stacy Giordano, with a hug. A curvy brunette with incredibly long legs, Stacy was glowing in her first trimester of pregnancy. Her wedding was scheduled for New Year's Eve in Texas, and Tess had used her contacts to arrange for a fabulous five-tiered cake.

"How's your little boy?" Tess asked.

"Doing better than I am. Morning sickness is no fun."

The last time they'd met, she and Stacy had talked about their kids, who were almost the same age. Stacy's son was autistic. "Did you bring him along on this trip?"

"He's here. We're staying with Lila's family at the Pierpont House in Arlington."

Tess's home and office were in Arlington, and she was familiar with the Pierpont—a Colonial-style mansion used by visiting dignitaries. The house came with its own maids and cooks. "Nice place. Has Governor Lockhart arrived?"

"Not yet. She won't be here until the day before the event. I came with Harlan." When she spoke the name of her fiancé, Stacy's cheeks flushed a bright, happy red. "He's setting up security at the Pierpont and for the event. His concerns are the reason for this meeting."

"How so?"

"He wants blueprints for the museum so he can check all entrances and exits, including the basement storage areas."

This request might be difficult to fulfill. Homeland Security got very nervous when it came to protecting national treasures like those that were housed in the museum. "I'm not sure if we can get clearance."

"Not even for Corps Security and Investigations?"

"If it was up to me, no problem."

Tess respected the reputation of CSaI, a private security firm based in Freedom, Texas. All the operatives were highly-trained, former military men. For the past several months while protecting Governor Lockhart, CSaI had dealt with death threats, bombings and snipers. From what Tess had heard, their actions had been competent and skillful.

The real reason she held CSaI in high regard was their founder—Bart Bellows. The 75-year-old Bellows was a Vietnam vet, a former CIA agent, a billionaire and the kindest man she'd ever known.

When Joe first went missing, Bellows had contacted her. Though he couldn't tell her Joe's assignment, he'd given her the impression that her husband had been vital in disarming a terrible threat to national security. Joe was a hero. But she'd already known that.

Instead of merely offering sympathy, Bart had stayed close to her for several days. In spite of his wheelchair, he'd helped in her catering kitchen. It was Bart who had notified her of Joe's death and arranged for him to be buried at Arlington. He'd also sorted through the mountains of paperwork to make sure she received the proper benefits and the payouts from other insurance policies. Bart had been with her in the hospital four months later when Joey was born.

She thought of him as her guardian angel, but he wasn't all sweetness and light. More than once, he'd dragged her out of depression and forced her to stand on her own two feet.

While acknowledging her grief, he encouraged her potential. Her move from catering into the more lucrative field of event planning came as a result of his contacts. In fact, he was the person who'd recommended her to Governor Lockhart.

For the past several weeks, Bart had been missing. When she thought of what might be happening to him, she shuddered. He was such a good man. Life truly was unfair. "Any news on Bart?"

"The guys have a couple of promising leads. If anyone can rescue him, they can."

Tess hoped and prayed that Stacy was right.

NOLAN LAW PEERED through his infrared, night vision goggles at an isolated flat-roof metal warehouse located eighteen miles outside Austin. A big, black Cadillac pulled up and parked outside the building. The Caddy cut its lights. Nobody got out.

From his surveillance position on a low ridge under the spreading branches of a live oak, Nolan could see a long way down the two-lane road leading to this warehouse. Another vehicle approached—an SUV. He parked behind the Caddy. Four armed men emerged and dispersed, setting up a perimeter at the four corners of the small warehouse with only one loading dock.

Through his ear bud, Nolan heard the smooth, calm voice of Wade Coltrane. "Is that everybody that's coming to the party?"

"Don't know." Nolan glanced to his left. He knew Coltrane was out there, but the man was invisible. "I didn't send out the invites."

The third man in their attack group, Nick Cavanaugh, said, "If we'd gotten here sooner, I could have set up some explosive charges inside."

"I should think you had enough of bombs," Nolan said. Last month, Cavanaugh and his lady had nearly been blown to bits by an explosive device in her son's day care center.

"I'm just saying," Cavanaugh muttered. "More time would have made this easier."

"Couldn't be helped." Nolan had gotten his intel from their CIA contact less than an hour ago. They'd been short on time, lucky to beat the Caddy and hide their Jeep in a gully behind the ridge.

The doors to the Caddy swung open. Two more bodyguards in dark windbreakers emerged from the front. From the back came a man in a suit with a white shirt that gleamed in the moonlight. On his arm was a blonde woman in a short, tight, red dress. Her presence was unexpected and would require an adjustment in strategy.

The suit and the woman went up the concrete stairs to an office door beside the loading dock and went inside. A single light over the door went on, casting a glow on the two men in windbreakers who stood directly outside.

"Hold your positions," Nolan said. "Let's give them half an hour to settle down."

The man in the suit was Robby Jessop, a shady defense contractor, who was likely using this warehouse to stash contraband weapons. Locating Jessop was the best lead CSaI had uncovered in their search for Bart Bellows, and Nolan didn't want to blow this opportunity.

He lowered himself to the ground and stretched out on his belly. On a night like this when the moon was half full, he wouldn't be seen with the naked eye. His dark cargo pants, jacket and dark knit cap blended into the shadows. But he wasn't taking any chances. One of the bodyguards might be smart enough to have night vision goggles of his own.

If it was the last thing he ever did, Nolan would find Bart Bellows. Over a month ago, the old man and his handicapped van had disappeared without a trace or a clue. His driver had been shot and killed, leaving no witness.

Nolan believed the old man was still alive. If Bart's enemies wanted him dead, they would have acted long before this. They'd kidnapped Bart for a reason and would hold him until they got what they wanted—whatever the hell that was.

The lack of apparent motive made CSaI's search intensely complicated. Bart had lived a long life and had ticked off a lot of scary people. Operating under the assumption that his abduction was related to his former career in the CIA, Nolan and the rest of the men in Corps Security and Investigations fought their way through a tangle of bureaucratic red tape to get secret documents declassified. They tracked down dozens of agents who could brief them on current situations that stemmed from Bart's former cases.

Nolan's best contact turned out to be a spy named Omar Harris who had his Irish-American father's sense of humor and his Afghani mother's courage. Omar gave him Jessop's name and told him that the defense contractor was involved in smuggling weapons and the opium trade in Afghanistan. It was Omar who arranged for Jessop to be at the warehouse outside Austin tonight. The defense contractor thought he was meeting with a warlord who would pay a cool million for their next deal.

Instead, Jessop was going to run into the three-man offense of Nolan, Coltrane and Cavanaugh—three former military men who had served with pride and distinction until they'd been recruited by Bart Bellows for his elite security company.

Poor little Robby Jessop didn't stand a chance.

Through his night vision goggles, Nolan scanned the area. The guard at the north side of the building was smoking a cigar. Both of the men nearest the warehouse door were texting on their cell phones.

None of them were paying attention.

All were distracted.

Taking them down would be cake.

"Are we ready?" Cavanaugh asked.

"I'll take the two men on the north side of the building," Nolan said. "You boys take care of the other side."

"What about the two by the door?"

"We'll use a flash-bang to get their attention, and then converge on them."

Nolan rolled onto his back and checked his weapons. The most dangerous part of this mission would be when they entered the warehouse. They were all wearing Kevlar, but Jessop would be waiting for them.

"Use your stun guns," Nolan said. "We're not here to kill anybody. We came to talk. Okay, let's rock and roll."

He crept through the night. Adrenaline pumped through his veins, heightening his senses and masking the ever-present ache from old wounds. He'd learned to endure the physical pain from injuries he'd suffered five years ago in Afghanistan, when his platoon was hit by a chopper strike and a roadside bomb. The emotional hurt was deeper, more intense, unrelieved by the passage of time.

Five years ago, Nolan Law had been a different man. Handsome and strong, his life had been filled with promise. His beautiful, loving wife had been pregnant. God, he missed Tess. He missed the son he'd never held in his arms, missed the life he should have had.

Nolan shook his head, pushing aside the regrets and the memories. There was no going back. He wasn't that man anymore. Joe Donovan was dead.

Chapter Two

Nolan circled the warehouse. The man on the far north side sat on the ground with his back leaning against the building. His gun was holstered, and his eyes were closed. Nolan deepened his nap with a blow that rendered him unconscious and then fastened the guard's wrists with a plastic tie.

The guy with the cigar was an equally easy takedown using a stun gun and a threat. "Make one sound and I'll shoot off your kneecap."

Nolan picked up the guard's gun—a sleek black repeating rifle in the newest generation of M40s. The fine weapon illustrated how being well-armed didn't matter as much as being well-disciplined. Any of the men in CSaI were capable of protecting a perimeter with nothing but a slingshot and a pocket knife.

As he moved to the corner of the warehouse, he heard a whisper from Cavanaugh, "We're in position."

"Do it."

When fired, a flash-bang emitted smoke, made a loud explosion and a blinding burst of light. The grenade-size device was more effective when used in an enclosed space, but the noise and flare would provide enough of a distraction for them to move on the guards at the front of the building.

Nolan averted his gaze so he wouldn't be blinded. As soon as he heard the bang, he ran at the guards. Before they could drop their cell phones and aim their weapons, the two men in dark windbreakers were down.

Nolan issued orders. "Cavanaugh, stay here, watch these guys. Coltrane, inside."

At the door to the warehouse, Nolan didn't hesitate. He kicked open the door, lobbed a smoke bomb inside and dove out of the way.

A volley of bullets from an automatic weapon sprayed through the doorway.

He heard the woman scream.

There was a lot of coughing. Another spurt of gunfire. More coughing.

Nolan and Coltrane used their infrared goggles to keep their vision clear. Coltrane held his rifle. Nolan had his stun gun and the guard's M40. They charged through the door into the warehouse.

It wasn't necessary to map out their strategy beforehand. They were both experienced military men who knew how to secure a building. Nolan went toward the right. Coltrane went left.

The warehouse was poorly lit with only a few bare bulbs. Through the smoke, Nolan saw an array of wooden crates, none of them stacked higher than his waist. Robby Jessop batted at the smoke and fired blindly. The woman had curled up on the concrete floor beside a desk.

"Who the hell are you?" Jessop yelled. "What do you want?"

Hiding behind crates, Nolan got within ten feet of Jessop before he made his move. It would have been tidier to zap him with the stun gun, but he wanted Jessop to be coherent and able to talk. That was the whole point.

When Jessop turned away from him, Nolan moved

fast. He delivered a rabbit punch to the kidneys, tore the weapon from Jessop's hands and knocked him face down onto the concrete. When he had Jessop's wrists secured, he pulled him up and marched him through the warehouse.

"Don't hurt me," Jessop wailed. "I can pay. Just don't hurt me."

He was a coward. Good. He'd be too scared to hold out.

It had already been agreed that Coltrane would take the lead in the interrogation. His specialty was infiltration into enemy situations. Not only did he know what questions to ask, but he was smooth enough to convince Jessop to trust him.

Nolan wasn't so glib, and his physical appearance was anything but charming. He didn't frighten little children, not anymore. But the facial reconstruction after his injuries had been extensive. He looked like a man who had been to hell and carried the scars.

While Cavanaugh kept watch over the six guards, Nolan brought Jessop around to the other side of his Caddy and shoved him down on his butt. "Don't move."

"I'm telling you," Jessop whined, "let me go and I'll make it worth your while."

Nolan traded places with Coltrane, taking custody of the woman in the tight red dress. He pushed his goggles up on his forehead and looked down at her. "You got a name?"

"Becky Joy." She glared up at him. Her eyes were red from the smoke bomb. "I have nothing to do with this guy. He was just a date."

"Take the woman," Jessop offered. "She's yours."

Angrily, she reacted. "You don't own me. You don't get to say who I belong to."

"Settle down." Nolan clamped his fingers around her wiry upper arm. "You won't be hurt."

Coltrane circled Jessop, who was sitting cross-legged in the dirt with his wrists fastened behind his back. Tears streaked down his cheeks. His shoulders shuddered as he gasped for breath. Jessop wasn't fat or skinny; he was as soft as a lump of pink clay. His formerly pristine white shirt was smudged and spattered with tiny drops of blood from a cut at the corner of his mouth.

In a calm voice, Coltrane lulled the defense contractor into a state of cooperation as he talked about the business of supplying weaponry for America and its allies in Iraq and Afghanistan. Without accusing, he hinted that maybe Jessop sold some of his guns to insurgents or warlords. And maybe, just maybe, there was a connection with the opium trade. "But mostly," Coltrane said, "you're providing supplies for our troops. You're a patriot."

"That's right." Jessop licked at the blood in the corner of his mouth. "You're military, aren't you?"

"What was your first clue?"

"The way you boys stormed into the warehouse. You've been trained. I can tell."

Disgusted, Nolan looked away. This marshmallow knew nothing about the military, except that he could make money selling guns. Coltrane's gentle approach was trying his patience.

"There was a guy in Iraq you might have known," Coltrane said. "Wes Bradley."

"Sure. He was one of my contacts."

"When was the last time you saw him?"

"Maybe six months ago," Jessop said. "Why? Are you looking for him? Is he the guy you're after?"

"Could be," Coltrane said.

Wes Bradley had been one of their primary suspects for the attacks on Governor Lockhart until they discovered that he'd been dead for over two years. Someone else was using his identity.

After Bart's abduction, they tested blood that supposedly belonged to Bradley and found a DNA match in the military database for Victor Bellows, Bart's son. But there was a problem with this identification. Victor had been stationed in Iraq and had been MIA for four years.

"I'll talk," Jessop said. "What do you want to know about Bradley?"

"Describe him."

"Over six feet, thinning brown hair. Not a bad looking guy but he has those crazy eyes. Know what I mean? Those pale blue eyes that seem to stare right through you."

Coltrane produced a high school photo of Victor Bellows. "Is this Wes Bradley?"

Jessop nodded. "He's older now, but that's him."

It was confirmation. Victor Bellows—Bart's only son—was involved in his father's abduction. Either Victor was the kidnapper or he knew who was holding his father.

"I've got another question," Coltrane said. "Do you know Bart Bellows?"

"I've heard the name." Jessop's manner shifted. He was edgy, not eager to talk about Bart. "He's a billionaire, right?"

"Don't play dumb with me," Coltrane said. "We're not here to enforce the law. But if you don't cooperate, we'll tell the CIA and Homeland Security about the weapons you're holding in this warehouse."

"If I talk, what do I get?"

Coltrane glanced over his shoulder at Nolan. "What can we offer?"

Nolan took out his cell phone. He had Omar Harris on speed dial. "As soon as I make this call, the CIA closes in. They'll confiscate your weapons, but that shouldn't be a problem for a patriot like you. These guns won't end up in the hands of insurgents or thugs. All I can give you is fifteen minutes head start before I make the call."

Jessop's eyes darted. "That's not much."

"Take it or leave it."

His mouth quivered. "There's something big going down. It has to do with a case Bellows investigated in Afghanistan. It's going to happen soon."

"When?" Coltrane demanded.

"The next couple of weeks. Washington, D.C., is the location."

Nolan felt a dark chill. Tess and his son lived in Arlington, too close to the threat. He held up his phone. "I need more. That's too vague."

"What do you mean?" Jessop wriggled, trying to free himself from the restraints.

"Something?" Nolan scoffed. "Something is happening in Washington? That's about as useful as telling me that Santa Claus is coming to town. If that's all you've got, I'm calling the law."

"Don't, please don't," Jessop begged. "I have a name. Just listen to me. The name is Greenaway."

A blade of ice sliced into Nolan's chest. Greenaway was the man who destroyed his life. Five years ago, Greenaway had threatened Tess and his unborn child. If he resurfaced, she was in imminent danger.

He had to find out more, had to stop Greenaway.

From the corner of his eye, Nolan saw the woman in the red dress moving. Too slowly, he turned toward her.

A gunshot exploded.

Blood spread across Jessop's chest. He fell to his side in the dirt.

The woman dropped her gun. Where the hell had she been hiding that weapon? Her dress was so damn tight that she could barely walk. She raised her hands. "You can arrest me. I don't care what happens."

Nolan hadn't expected this, hadn't been prepared. "Why?"

"Jessop killed my mother. The bastard deserves to die."

But not yet. Not when Jessop had information Nolan needed.

The possibility that Greenaway was involved changed the focus of Nolan's search for Bart. He needed to be in Washington, D.C., as soon as possible, and he had to make certain that Tess was safe.

THE OFFICE FOR Donovan Event Planning was a small store-front near Ballston Common Mall in Arlington. After dropping Joey off at day care, Tess arrived at a few minutes after ten in the morning. She hung her burgundy coat and the jacket of her black pantsuit in the closet and went to the sleek Plexiglas front desk where she sat and closed her eyes for a two-minute meditation.

Getting herself and her son ready in the morning took a lot of energy. Though Joey liked playing with the other kids at his day care, she always felt a twinge of guilt about leaving him. It had never been her intention to be a single mother.

She inhaled through her nostrils and exhaled through her mouth. In her mind, she pictured a blue horizon above a still body of water. Clouds blew in, and the sky and sea faded to the white of a blank slate. A fresh start.

With her eyes refreshed, she rose from the desk and looked with pride at her clean line, modern office. The pale blue walls were hung with clear-framed photos of events, awards and a couple of personal pictures. The chairs at either end of the long white leather sofa were royal purple and lime green.

She enjoyed meeting with clients in this area where she wowed them with old-fashioned scrapbooks of prior events and a brand-new digital presentation that outlined her capabilities.

Behind a half-wall partition at the back of the office was the casual break room with a fridge, a counter and a little round table. There was also a play area for Joey, file cabinets and a scheduling board. Tess went to the coffee maker and got the first pot of the day started.

She heard the front door open and peeked around the partition. Her sense of serenity took an immediate hit when she confronted a muscular man with thick, curly black hair. Pierre LeBrune was the head chef for the catering company she was using for the Lockhart Christmas Eve event. Though he didn't have an accent and probably wasn't really from France, he dressed in splendid European style from his silk necktie to his flashy platinum Patek Philippe wristwatch.

She didn't dare offer him her less-than-perfect coffee. "Good morning, Chef."

"We have a problem, Mrs. Donovan."

It wasn't the first. Pierre had popped up at her office a half-dozen times over the past three months to nitpick. The company he owned with two partners was one of the top-notch caterers in Washington, D.C., and it was the first time she'd worked with them.

Usually Tess used the catering service she'd founded, but the Smithsonian insisted she choose from a list of caterers they had worked with before. Though inconvenient for her, she understood that all the cooks and servers needed security clearance to work after hours in the National Museum of American History, where so many patriotic artifacts were on display.

She gestured to the sofa. "Would you like to sit?"

He sneered at the furniture as though the white leather upholstery wasn't good enough for him. "I won't be here long. I have a problem with the meat supplier."

"You have a beef with the beef?"

Ignoring her attempt to lighten the mood, he glared. "I prefer using my regular butcher. This Texas beef doesn't rise to my standards."

"I'm sorry, Chef. Our client is the governor of Texas, and she specified the supplier." She added a compliment. "I know Governor Lockhart is looking forward to your sage-encrusted prime rib."

He managed to preen and scowl at the same time. "What about the poultry supplier?"

"Also specifically requested. You'll have to find a way to use free-range Texas chickens."

"This is unacceptable. I have a reputation."

He most certainly did. Everyone had told Tess that Pierre was a royal pain in the butt. "I'm sure you'll find a way to please the client. Did you know that she's being seriously considered as a candidate for president?"

"Oh." His thick eyebrows lifted. "I had no idea."

"Just be glad she didn't demand barbecue," she said. "You're a culinary legend, Pierre. You'll find a way to make this work."

"Indeed, I will."

He pivoted and left.

Had she bitten off more than she could chew with this super fancy sit-down dinner? An evening at the Smithsonian wasn't her style. As her office manager, Trudy Benson, often reminded her, Donovan Event Planning was best suited to arranging birthday parties with clowns and petting zoos.

Expanding her business to include more sophisticated events was a good move financially, but it wasn't easy.

In a city where everything was measured in terms of influence and leverage, she had zero clout. Yesterday, the events coordinator at the Smithsonian had no trouble turning down her request to see the blueprints. If Tess was going to change her mind, she needed somebody important on her side. Bart Bellows would have been perfect for the job. He could have used his CIA contacts.

The minute she thought of using Bart, she was ashamed of herself. He'd been missing for weeks. Her little problems were nothing compared to what he was going through. God, she hoped he was all right.

She filled her coffee mug and checked out the huge whiteboard where Trudy kept the monthly schedule updated. Five days before Christmas, the Smithsonian dinner was the only event for the week. Next week, she had two small New Year's Eve parties. Today, Tess would meet a client at lunchtime to plan a dinner party in January.

When she heard the front door open, she poured black coffee into Trudy's mug and stepped around the partition. "Thank goodness, you're here. I need your help."

The person who had entered wasn't perky, gray-haired Trudy Benson. He was the opposite. A tall, husky man in black slacks, a gray turtleneck and a black leather jacket, he was solid, powerful and totally masculine. Though he wore dark aviator glasses, she felt him staring at her.

Soundlessly, he crossed the floor and took the coffee mug from her hand. When his fingers brushed hers, electricity sparked between them. The buzz surprised her. It had been years since she'd felt that kind of reaction to a man.

She licked her lips. "You're not Trudy."

"But I'd be happy to help you. In any way I can."

His low, raspy voice vibrated in the air between them. In that instant, Tess decided that he was the sexiest man she'd ever met. He wasn't handsome in the conventional way. His face was rugged and scarred. His brow was heavy, and his nose looked like it had been smashed with a hammer.

She stammered, "Who are you?"

"Nolan Law."

The name was familiar, but she couldn't place it. She held out her hand as she introduced herself. "I'm Tess Donovan."

His grasp was firm. His hand was rough and calloused. His touch increased the spark she'd felt into a thousand-volt shock. She was actually trembling. "C-c-can I help you?"

"I'm handling security for Governor Lockhart's event."

"I thought Stacy's fiancé was in charge."

"The situation merits my attention," he said. "With Bart gone, I'm in charge."

Yes, you are. She'd take orders from Mr. Law any day of the week.

Chapter Three

When Trudy dashed through the front door of the office, Tess mentally pushed her back outside. She wanted more alone time with Nolan. His presence validated all those resolutions she'd made about moving on with her life.

"Bad news," Trudy said as she hung her coat in the closet near the door. "That stuffed gopher my baby grandson wants for Christmas is nowhere to be found. I'm thinking I could chop the ears off a bunny and it might do."

Pushing her curly gray hair into shape, she darted toward them, introduced herself to Nolan and tilted her head back to look up at him. "You're a former marine. Am I right?"

"Yes, ma'am."

"I can always tell." Her blue eyes twinkled. In her lace blouse with the sparkly Christmas-tree brooch, Trudy Benson was the very definition of cute little old lady. "My oldest boy was in the Corps for ten years before he settled down. Where were you stationed?"

"That information's classified," he said.

"You can tell me. It's not like I'm a terrorist, even if I do have to take my shoes off at the airport. I'll just assume it was the Middle East. Do you speak Farsi or Arabic?"

"Both."

For a moment, Tess considered letting Trudy continue

with her questions. Her adorable grandma persona gave her free rein to say things that would have sounded rude coming from anyone else, and Tess was curious about Nolan.

But she didn't want to waste his time. "Mr. Law is handling security for the event at the Smithsonian."

"I should have guessed," Trudy said. "Corps Security and Investigations, the business that Bart Bellows founded. Is there any word on Bart?"

Tess stared into Nolan's dark glasses. She hoped to hear something positive but feared the worst.

"I'm sorry," Nolan said. "Nothing new."

She sensed that he was holding back. Later, she'd push for more details. "I'm glad you're here, Mr. Law. We have a problem with the security."

"We're going to be working together, Tess. Call me Nolan."

His rasping voice struck an unusual note. At the same time, his cadence and pronunciation sounded familiar. "All right, Nolan. About this problem…"

"The blueprints at the Smithsonian," he said. "I have a contact who can obtain the necessary security clearance. He needs to meet you."

"When?"

"Now would be good." He checked his wristwatch. "I'll drive."

Though she didn't have pressing matters to handle this morning, Tess wasn't a big fan of the spontaneous. She liked to have things planned and executed with tidy precision. "I have a meeting at one o'clock."

"I'd be happy to drive you there," he said.

"Excuse me for a moment."

She took Trudy's arm and retreated behind the partition. As soon as she was out of Nolan's view, Tess exhaled a breath she hadn't been aware of holding. Her heart was beating faster. She felt warm all over. She whispered, "I can't just drop everything and waltz out the door with him. Can I?"

"You really must." Trudy patted her shoulder. "Nolan Law is the hottest thing that's been in this office since we did a test run with that thirtieth birthday cake with all the sparklers and the tablecloth caught on fire."

"May I remind you that we had to replace a chair after that disaster?"

"Are you sweating?" Trudy asked. "Am I seeing a sheen of perspiration?"

"No." But yes, she was. Her forehead was damp.

"For goodness sakes, Tess. Go with the sexy bodyguard. If anybody deserves some zing in their life, it's you."

Tess wiped her palms on her black slacks and tried to gather her composure. "He's definitely sexy."

"He's kind of a thug with all those scars, but there's something about him. It's pretty doggoned obvious that you like him."

"For all I know, he might be happily married."

"Oops, I hadn't thought of that." Trudy pivoted. "Let's find out."

Before Tess could stop her, Trudy darted around the partition and up to Nolan. He was standing at the front desk, holding a clear-framed snapshot of Tess's son at the top of a slide waving his hands in the air. He held up the picture. "Is this your boy?"

She nodded. "That's Joey. He's four."

"I can see the resemblance to you."

"Not really," she said. "He's the image of his father, healthy and funny and more headstrong than is good for him."

Trudy piped up, "Do you like children, Nolan?"

"Yes."

Trudy beamed her grandmotherly smile. "Have you started your own family yet? Is there a Mrs. Nolan Law?"

"A missus?" He seemed amused by the concept. "Actually, there is no Mrs. Nolan Law."

"No time like the present to get started," Trudy said. "You two should get going. I'll take care of the office."

Tess started to object. "But I—"

"If anything comes up, I'll call or email or text. Run along."

Feeling like she'd been railroaded by the Trudy bullet train, Tess slipped into her suit jacket and coat, grabbed her briefcase with the laptop inside and followed Nolan out the door. She expected a rugged man like him to drive a Hummer. Instead, he had a classic black Mercedes.

She buckled her seat belt and leaned back in the luxurious seat. "Where are we headed?"

"A café in D.C.," he said. "This meeting shouldn't take more than a couple of minutes."

"I'd like to apologize for Trudy being so intrusive."

"Not at all," he said. "She reminds me of my late grandma. A Southern belle who knew everything about everybody in her little town. Grandma always said she wasn't nosy. Just concerned."

Aha! He had Southern roots. "I thought I heard a hint of an accent. Did you grow up in the South?"

"I've lived all over. You?"

"I grew up in a suburb of Chicago. My dad was a police officer, killed in the line of duty." She pinched her lips together. She wanted information from him, not the other way around.

He asked, "What brought you to Arlington?"

"College. I wanted to be an art historian but got sidetracked along the way by the culinary arts." And by Joe

Donovan. Instead of going to graduate school, she'd married him and launched her career as a caterer.

"Any regrets about dropping the career in art?"

"None," she said quickly. "I chose the right path."

Even though she'd lost Joe, the love they'd shared was true and deep. She'd experienced the kind of passion that poets write about. Not that she and Joe were gooey and sentimental. His greatest talent had been making her laugh. More than anything else, he had wanted her to be happy. If Joe could see her now, he'd tell her to give Nolan a chance. She glanced toward him, wondering if he'd ever take off those sunglasses.

Nolan said, "Bart mentioned that your son was born after your husband went missing. That must have been rough."

"My son's birth was the high point of my life, and I wish with all my heart that my husband could have shared that moment when I first heard Joey cry." She couldn't help smiling when she recalled the joy and relief she'd felt when she held her perfectly formed, newborn baby boy. Joey was so full of energy, wriggling and waving his arms. It was a wonderful moment. But she didn't want to talk about herself. "Bart was with me. He's a very special part of our lives. I'd like to know more about his abduction."

"Such as?"

"Start at the beginning."

"There was an explosion at a day care center," he said. "In the confusion, Bart was taken. His handicap van was missing, and his driver was killed."

Tess had heard this part of the story. "It seems like his van could be traced. Did it have GPS?"

"There were tracking devices in both the van and Bart's motorized wheelchair. Both were deactivated immediately.

We found the van about a week later. A bomb had been exploded inside. There was no useful evidence."

"And no contact from the kidnappers," she said. "I know Bart sees his doctors on a regular basis and is on a regimen of medications."

"None of his prescriptions have been used, but his meds are fairly common, easily purchased. None of his regular docs have heard from the people who kidnapped him."

"I worry that he's not being properly cared for."

Nolan's jaw tensed. The long scar that stretched from the edge of his nose to his earlobe defined his cheekbone. "I can't promise you that Bart is all right. We don't have any definite leads, and I don't like to speculate."

She sensed that he was trying to shelter her from worry as though she was a delicate hothouse orchid. Such concerns were unnecessary. She'd been through a lot of pain in her life, starting with the death of her father when she was in her teens. The other cops on the force had tried to protect her and her mother by not talking about the way he died, but the closed casket pretty much said it all. Her dad had been shot point-blank in the face by a low-life drug dealer who was currently spending life in prison.

Her mom refused to face what had happened, but Tess attended the trial for the drug dealer. Every single day in court, she stared at the bastard who killed her dad, and she experienced every shade of rage and hatred. Dealing with Joe's death was more difficult; she couldn't focus her anger and sadness on a faceless enemy.

"I can handle the truth," she said. "I'd rather know everything than not enough. You've been investigating for nearly a month. I assume you have suspects."

He turned toward her. His eyes were hidden by the dark glasses, but she could feel his gaze. "You're stronger than you look."

"I'm going to take that as a compliment. Now, talk."

"There's a possibility that Bart was abducted by his son, Victor Bellows."

She was surprised. "I didn't know Bart had any children."

"He was estranged from his son."

That didn't seem like Bart at all. He was ferociously loyal and caring; he'd be a great father. "There's more to that story."

"That's what I'm trying to figure out," Nolan said. "Bart's son went into the military when he was eighteen. He did a tour in Iraq and got into trouble with the military police. Rather than be incarcerated, he went AWOL. The military classified him as MIA."

"How did you find out he was still alive?"

"Victor was using an alias. We found blood at the site of the abduction. When we ran tests, we found a DNA match through the army database."

A father kidnapped by his own son? She hated to think of the betrayal. There must be another answer. "The fact that his blood was at the scene doesn't prove that Victor is the kidnapper. He might have been trying to protect his father. Like you, he might be searching for Bart right now."

"Anything's possible." But Nolan sounded skeptical.

"I know Bart was in the CIA for a long time," she said. "He must have a lot of enemies."

"True."

"If Victor took him, he might be keeping his father out of sight to protect him." She wanted to believe that Bart's son wouldn't hurt him. "How much do you know about Victor Bellows?"

"Under his alias, he was involved in some bad stuff. It's hard to believe that Bart's son would grow up to be a criminal, but that's what it looks like." He paused to take a breath. "I have reason to believe that Victor is here in Washington."

"That's the actual reason you're in town, isn't it? If you weren't looking for Victor Bellows, you would have left security for Governor Lockhart's event to Stacy's fiancé."

"Not necessarily."

"What other reason could there be?"

"Maybe I came here to meet you."

Was he flirting with her? Tess had been out of the dating game for such a long time that she barely recognized the signs of male attention. "To meet me? Why? What have you heard?"

"I might have heard that you're a charming woman with black hair and eyes like sapphires. Someone might have told me that you're creative, smart and efficient. According to rumors, you're the total package. You can even cook."

She felt her jaw drop. "Is that so?"

"Thus far, I'm not disappointed." A grin twitched the corner of his mouth. "But I haven't tasted your mushroom and asparagus risotto."

How did he know that was her best dish? When she was working as a caterer, she could always count on her risotto. Apparently, he knew more about her than she did about him. That disparity had to end.

Near the Marine Memorial, he merged onto a main route to cross the Teddy Roosevelt Bridge. Nolan drove like someone who was familiar with D.C. and Arlington. "Doesn't look like you need directions," she said.

"I've spent time in this area."

"At the Pentagon?" she guessed.

He shrugged and said nothing. Pulling information from him was like plucking tail feathers from a chicken. He seemed determined to maintain an aura of mystery, which should have been irritating. Instead, she was intrigued.

Gazing through the windshield at gray skies, she said, "Cloudy day. Do you really need those sunglasses or are they a necessary accessory for security men?"

Another grin. "Are you teasing me, Tess?"

"I dare you to take them off."

He stopped for a red light, turned to her and whipped off the dark glasses. For less than five seconds, his gaze met hers. Then the sunglasses were back in place as his attention returned to the traffic.

She wasn't so quick to recover. Shocked, she jolted back in her seat. She was drowning, struggling to catch her breath. Why was this happening to her again? Was she losing her mind?

In Nolan's eyes, she saw a ghost.

Her fingers clenched, and she dug her nails into her palms, hoping the stab of pain would wake her from this insane illusion. It wasn't possible. Joe Donovan was dead.

Chapter Four

As they drove onto the Teddy Roosevelt Bridge, Tess was aware of the other vehicles, the heavy clouds and the dark waters of the Potomac. But she saw them all in a blur. She heard herself speaking but had no idea what she'd said.

Nolan's eyes were a dark gray, more deep set than Joe's but exactly the same color. Nolan's left eye was a few centimeters lower than the right. He wasn't perfectly handsome, wasn't her darling husband. And yet, in those few seconds when she'd looked into the windows to his soul, she saw Joe Donovan.

"Tess? Are you all right?"

His raspy voice—unlike Joe's clear baritone—called to her. She needed to respond. Didn't want him to think she was a nutcase even though there was no other explanation. "Headache," she said. "I have a little headache."

He was immediately solicitous. "Should I take you home?"

"No."

He drove past Foggy Bottom toward Georgetown University, the place where she and Joe had met. Whispers of the past tickled her ears, telling her that she'd found the love of her life. *That could not be.* Nolan wasn't Joe. She couldn't allow herself to confuse the two. Their eyes were similar. So what? Lots of men had gray eyes.

More firmly, she said, "I'm fine. My stomach will be fine."

"I thought it was your head."

"Whatever."

Thankfully, they drove past the turnoff to the university. If he'd pulled up in front of the coffee shop where she and Joe had spent hours together when they were dating, she might have gone into full-blown fantasy mode, imagining herself as a wide-eyed college student who'd fallen madly in love with a handsome marine. That wasn't her. Not anymore.

Tess had a new identity, a satisfying identity. First and foremost, she was Joey's mom. Then, she was a businesswoman who needed to show the man driving this slick Mercedes that she was responsible and merited referrals.

Swallowing her confusion, she pulled herself together. The smart thing would be to avoid any further interaction with Nolan. No sidelong glances. No flirting. Most definitely, she wouldn't touch the man. Pretending calm, she asked, "Who is the person we're meeting?"

"His name is Omar Harris. He's a friend of Bart's."

"A spy?"

"CIA," Nolan said. "He'll arrange for our clearance so we can take a look at the blueprints for the museum."

"Why did he need to see me?"

"Covering his bases. You'll have to give him the name of your events coordinator at the Smithsonian."

Though she wasn't quite sure why she needed face time with this person, Tess didn't ask for further explanation. A lot of the protocols in Washington were absurdly complicated.

Nolan found a parking place at the curb in a neighborhood of storefronts. The tree branches were lined with fairy lights that were lit even though it was daylight.

The shop windows featured colorful Christmas decorations—snowflakes, tinsel and big red bows. A bell-ringer on the corner solicited contributions. Instead of waiting for him to come around and open her door, Tess climbed out quickly. She didn't want to risk having Nolan take her hand to help her.

He stepped onto the sidewalk beside her. "Is something wrong?"

"Not at all." Avoiding eye contact, she glanced at her gold wristwatch. "I'm concerned about making it to my other meeting on time. It might be best if I catch a cab."

"I'll drive you. I insist."

When he touched her elbow to guide her down the street, she flinched. He backed off, giving her plenty of space. Had she insulted him? She wanted to create the opposite effect, but she was scared. Given the choice between too close and too far, she opted for distance.

Halfway down the block, he opened the door to the Minuteman Café and held it for her. Inside, the decor was red-white-and-blue homey with half-curtains on the windows, a long counter, brown leatherette booths and a silver tinsel Christmas tree by the cash register. The lunch rush hadn't started, and there were only a few patrons. Which of these men was the spy? Was it the silver-haired gentleman? The guy in the black trench coat?

Nolan went to a booth at the rear of the diner to greet Omar Harris. Dressed in sneakers, gray sweatpants and an insulated Georgetown hoodie, he looked like a jogger. His curly black hair was sprinkled with gray. His features were ordinary, which, she supposed, was a plus for a spy.

After Nolan introduced them, he slid into the booth, leaving room for her. She had no choice but to sit beside Nolan with their thighs only inches apart. Using her briefcase, she created a barrier between them.

Omar sipped from his coffee mug. "I recommend the Minuteman blueberry muffins."

"None for me." She'd had a big waffle and sausage breakfast with Joey. "How's the coffee?"

"Passable." Omar signaled to the waitress.

Nolan stretched his arm across the back of the booth, and she leaned forward to avoid making contact. Her neatly folded hands rested on the tabletop. "Is there any information you need from me, Mr. Harris?"

"I've already run a background check."

Of course, he had. The CIA probably knew more about her than she knew herself. "Did you find anything interesting?"

Though his clothes were casual, his manner turned sharp. His dark eyes riveted on her in a piercing gaze. "Where are you sending your son to school?"

Taken aback, she sputtered, "What?"

"I have an eighteen-month-old. My wife and I are trying to decide where he should go to school. Any ideas?"

"You?" Nolan said. "I didn't know you had a baby."

Omar raked his fingers through his graying hair. "I know I'm a little old to be a first-time dad."

"Second wife?" Nolan asked.

"Number three. The third time is a charm. I couldn't be happier." He turned back to her. "Any suggestions?"

"I love our neighborhood in Arlington," she said. "When we bought our house, we checked into the public schools. I'm happy with that option."

"You bought your home with your husband," Nolan said. "Joe Donovan."

"Yes." Once again, Joe was front and center. She'd thought about him more in the past twenty-four hours than she had in the last month.

"I'm sorry for your loss," Omar said. "Your husband

was a hero. If you don't mind my asking, how did he come to know Bart Bellows?"

"I'm not sure. Bart never really explained. He showed up on my doorstep, took my hand and helped me through the most difficult time of my life. Honestly, I don't know how I would have managed without him."

"You never knew why," Omar said.

She shook her head. "I know I'm not the only one he's helped through a rough time."

"That's the truth," Omar said. "Bart has dedicated his life and his wealth to helping veterans returning from war, giving them a jump start on a new life. That's the idea behind Corps Security and Investigations. Right, Nolan?"

"CSaI is more than a job. We're brothers."

Though Tess didn't know the backgrounds of the men who formed CSaI, Bart had spoken of the pain they'd suffered. She knew how proud he was of these veterans. Bart's intense concern for others made his relationship with his son even more difficult to understand. Why was he estranged from Victor? Why hadn't he been able to help his only child?

FIVE YEARS AGO, Nolan had faced the prospect of never seeing his wife or his child again. His enemies had been watching Tess and Joey. If they had any idea that Joe Donovan was still alive, his family would suffer the consequences. At the time, Nolan had thought there was no greater pain than separation. He'd been wrong. Today, spending time with Tess, was sheer torture.

When she'd looked into his eyes and then turned away in disgust, a molten dagger sliced into his gut. He was ashamed of what he had become. His scars made him grotesque—unworthy of her. Beauty and the beast was a damn fairy tale. In real life, the pretty people stuck together while monsters like him hid in the shadows.

On the street, when he'd touched her elbow, she had cringed. In the café, she'd used her briefcase to build a wall between them. Though she'd tried to be polite, it had been pretty damned clear that she wanted nothing to do with him.

The rejection seared his soul, burning away the thick protective shields he used to keep his distance from anyone who tried to get too close. He must never let Tess know that Nolan Law was, in fact, her beloved Joe. It was better for her to remember him with fondness than to face the god-awful truth.

Meeting his son was bound to open an even deeper wound. Kids weren't hampered by manners; they pointed at him and hid their faces in their mother's skirts. In the early days before his burns and facial reconstruction had healed, Nolan couldn't stand being out in public. His appearance was better now. After more surgeries than he could count, he looked almost normal. But not normal enough; his face was still distorted enough to drive Tess away from him.

What the hell had he expected? That she'd take one look at him and leap into his arms? No such happy ending was possible for him.

Though he wanted to run from her and hide himself in a dark cave where he could lick his wounds, solitude wasn't the answer. The minute Jessop mentioned Greenaway, Nolan knew the threat had returned. He had to put aside his feelings and dedicate himself to protecting her and Joey.

The main reason he'd wanted Tess to meet Omar was so that he could gauge the other man's reaction to the mention of Joe Donovan. Nobody, except for Bart, knew that

Nolan was Joe. Keeping his identity and the fact that he'd survived was vital to the safety of his wife and child.

Omar had passed the test. Though the longtime CIA operative had been trained to conceal his reactions, Nolan's perceptions were razor sharp. He had sensed no interest from Omar in Joe Donovan.

Nolan wished he hadn't promised to escort Tess to her next meeting. He was anxious for this misery to end, and it took every tattered shred of his self-control to behave in the cool, collected manner that befitted a marine. Remaining civil was killing him by inches. Combat would have been easier.

After they left the café and were back in the Mercedes, he tried to fill the uncomfortable silence. "Tell me about the people we're going to see."

"The Zamir family," she said, "is filthy rich and socially connected at the highest level. The three daughters are always dressed head-to-toe in designer fashion, even the fourteen-year-old. The father has a diplomatic post in the Royal Saudi Embassy, but I don't think it's a real job. Just a title."

Nolan trusted her instincts. He always had. "Why do you think he's lying?"

"I wouldn't go so far as to say it's a lie. Mr. Zamir's connection to the embassy is a convenience while he's handling his other business."

Keeping his focus on the traffic around them, he stole a glance at her. Her shoulder-length black hair fell forward, obscuring his view of her lovely face. Her slender fingers laced in her lap, and he noticed that she still wore her platinum wedding band. She'd moved it from her left hand to her right, but it was still there. She hadn't forgotten him.

He cleared his throat. "What's Zamir's real business?"

"I have no idea. This town is so full of intrigue that the truth is little more than a rumor."

He didn't like the idea of Tess being swept up in one of these intrigues. "How did you meet these clients?"

"You have a lot of questions."

"I'm an investigator," he said. "Did you meet the Zamirs through Bart?"

"A lot of my clients were referrals from Bart, but I met the Zamir family a long time ago when I was catering. They use high-profile event planners most of the time, but I'm the one they call for last-minute things. Like this dinner for ten in January."

Though her explanation was plausible, he couldn't help having suspicions. Bart's kidnapping had opened the door to long-buried dangers. "It's not a problem if I accompany you inside, is it?"

"Well, I don't usually travel with a bodyguard, but I'll introduce you as a friend. You're not going to believe the inside of their house."

"Why is that?" He glanced toward her again. Though she wasn't looking at him, she was grinning.

"The Zamirs have tons of stuff. All of it glitters. Their decor is incredibly ornate—gold-leaf furniture, polished brass vases and crystal chandeliers."

"Snazzy."

He heard her gasp, and he knew he'd used the wrong word. Whenever she described something that was over-the-top, she called it snazzy.

"You're right." Her voice was breathless. "Snazzy is exactly what I would say."

He cursed himself for being careless. An apology would only make it worse. He drove in silence. The air inside the Mercedes clouded with suppressed emotion. There was so much he wanted and needed to say. Even if he tried to explain, he didn't know where to start.

The GPS navigator in the Mercedes had directed him into an upscale, exclusive neighborhood. "We're getting close," he said.

She reached over and rested her arm on his shoulder. "Would you pull over? Just for a moment."

Her touch suffused him with a warm glow. Clearly, she had no idea of the effect she had on him. Tess had always been unaware of her own beauty.

As he parked at the curb, he steeled himself. "What is it, Tess?"

"We seem to have gotten off on the wrong foot." When she frowned, her eyebrows crinkled. "I want to apologize."

He knew she was trying to be polite. Though her reaction to his ugliness was natural, she didn't want to offend. "You don't have to say you're sorry."

"Let me explain, please. I'm not usually so tongue-tied and clumsy. My event-planning business is largely based on my ability to get along with people, and I've got to clear the air." She stared into his sunglasses. "I know this is a cliché, but it's not you. It's me."

"Okay."

"You remind me of someone," she said, "someone who was very dear to me. It doesn't make sense. You don't look like him. And your tone of voice is different. But there's… a certain something. Being with you is bringing back a whole lot of memories that are…inappropriate."

He couldn't believe what she was saying. She'd recognized him. In spite of everything, she had known in her heart that he was her husband. By God, he loved this woman.

"It's all right, Tess. I understand."

"How could you?"

"I've lost someone, too."

And he would find a way to win her back.

Chapter Five

Inside the Zamir mansion, Nolan was glad to be wearing his dark glasses. Tess's description of the garish, snazzy decor had been accurate. She had, however, failed to mention the several mirrors and reflective surfaces. As always, Nolan avoided looking at himself. He focused instead on Tess as she approached the lady of the house and a stunning young woman who had to be her daughter. All three ladies were slim with black hair, but that was where the similarity ended. Both Zamirs were olive-skinned with dramatic makeup and strong features. Tess had a porcelain complexion with pink roses in her cheeks. Her bright blue eyes with naturally thick lashes needed very little makeup.

After Tess introduced him, they went down the hallway to a long, polished table under two sparkly chandeliers. Green chai tea that reminded him of Afghanistan was served in tiny, ornate china cups. He halfway listened as the women discussed the small dinner party that would be taking place in a few weeks.

Their meeting gave every appearance of an everyday transaction for an event planner, but Nolan sensed an undercurrent. Did the Zamirs have something to hide?

He inserted himself into the conversation. "Your home is beautiful, Mrs. Zamir. You have elegant taste."

"Thank you." Her full lips parted in a smile. "My

daughter thinks I should scale back. She likes the plain, boring modern style."

"Just for myself," said the younger woman who was dressed in a snug turquoise top with silver embroidery at the plunging neckline. "Glitz suits you, Mama."

Nolan said, "Tess mentioned that you met her when she was a caterer."

"Her orange truffles brought us together," Mrs. Zamir said. "My husband tasted those chocolates at a dinner he attended and asked me to try Tess. I have never been disappointed."

Nolan's suspicions deepened. The husband had arranged the contact with Tess. Her shift from catering to event planning was six months after Joey was born—a time that coincided with speculation that Joe Donovan might still be alive. He had to wonder if the Zamirs were using Tess because of her friendship with Bart.

A tall man entered from the kitchen. He was dressed from head to toe in black, making him look even thinner than he was. Mrs. Zamir introduced him as her husband's nephew, Ben. When they shook hands, Nolan sized him up. A handshake could be a useful measure of character. Some men turned it into a macho test of strength. Others pumped nervously.

Nephew Ben's handshake was like the sting of a scorpion—quick and lethal. His upper lip curled in a sneer as he asked, "What is your occupation?"

Nolan guessed that Ben already knew who he was. To lie would make him appear suspicious. "I'm in town to provide security for Governor Lockhart of Texas."

"Oh," said Mrs. Zamir. "There are those who want the governor to run for president. Why are you with Tess?"

"I'm planning the governor's Christmas Eve party at

the Smithsonian," Tess explained. "Nolan and I have been working out some of the details."

Mrs. Zamir and her daughter reacted with squeals of excitement. Private events at the Smithsonian were a big deal, and they were delighted to be using an event planner who was part of such a prestigious event.

"If you don't mind my asking," the daughter said, "how were you selected? Are you friends with the Lockharts?"

"It was a referral," Tess said. "Do you know Bart Bellows?"

Behind his dark glasses, Nolan kept a watchful eye on the nephew. At the mention of Bart's name, a muscle in his jaw twitched. In the depths of his dark eyes was a glimmer of hatred. "Corps Security and Investigations," Ben said. "That's the company founded by Bellows."

"Correct," Nolan said. "He's my boss."

Less than two minutes later, Ben excused himself and left the room. Nolan wanted to follow him, to see who he was reporting to, but he assumed there was surveillance inside this mansion and didn't want to behave in a manner that would draw further attention to himself. So, he settled back in his chair and stayed with the ladies.

As the women analyzed every detail of the upcoming dinner party, he tuned out. There was only so much discussion of food and cutlery that he could take. Did it really matter if the orchid table decorations were mauve or magenta? Was asparagus in season? Which vintage wine was the best?

His gaze rested on Tess. She was animated, engaging, charming. Her head tilted to the right when she listened. Tiny dimples appeared in her cheeks when she chuckled. Her laughter enchanted him, and he remembered going to great lengths to amuse her. He'd told jokes and surprised her with silly presents. In the early days of their lovemaking, he'd bought a pack of neon condoms so they could play hide-and-seek in the dark.

In the bedroom. Remembering her in his bed was a mistake, but he couldn't stop himself from thinking about Tess stretched out on the cream-colored sheets with one hand tangled in her silky black hair and her other arm reaching toward him. She had an exotic floral scent that reminded him of jasmine. He remembered the graceful curve of her hips, her tiny waist and her perfect breasts that she thought were too small. She was the most beautiful woman he'd ever seen.

And he had to stop thinking about her. He couldn't afford distractions. Not when there was the potential for danger in this very house.

He rose from the table and asked for directions to the restroom. Back to the foyer and down the hall to the right, it was the first door. He walked slowly, getting his bearings. The foyer was two stories tall with beveled glass windows on each side of the double front door. To his right was a curving staircase with marble banister and a toga-draped goddess statue standing where the newel post should have been.

From the gallery above his head, Nolan overheard a conversation, male voices speaking Arabic. He was familiar enough with the language to catch the gist of what they were saying. They were talking about Bart. One man said that Bart Bellows had vanished and speculated that he might be in hiding. The other—who sounded like nephew Ben—mentioned the presence of CSaI operatives. He said that Nolan was Bellow's *ghul,* referring to a monster from Arabian folklore, a ghoul.

Nolan liked the characterization. A *ghul* should be feared. And a *ghul* sure as hell wasn't the handsome Joe Donovan.

The men were walking on the open galley above his head, moving out of earshot. The last thing he heard clearly was a mention of Wes Bradley—the alias that Bart's son had been using for years. Wes Bradley had warned them, had told them that Bart wanted to disrupt their plans.

Nolan's suspicions were confirmed. The Zamir family had contacted Tess because of her friendship with Bart. She was being drawn into a web of danger.

His first instinct was to protect her. But how could he become her bodyguard without telling her how and why she was in danger? He wouldn't lie to Tess, but he wasn't ready to reveal his identity.

In the ornate bathroom with gold faucets, embroidered towels and gold cherub soap dishes, he took out his cell phone. Initially, the plan had been for him and Harlan to coordinate the security for Governor Lockhart while continuing the search for Bart. More backup was necessary. Nolan needed to call the CSaI office in Freedom, Texas, and get the rest of the men up here ASAP.

He wasn't sure what kind of reception he'd get from this bathroom tucked inside a mansion, but he was confident that no one could read his signal. Bart had provided him with an untraceable cell phone.

His call was answered on the first ring by Amelia Bond, who started with an accusation. "Nolan, you haven't checked in at the hotel yet."

"Is that a problem? Are you getting some kind of discount or something?"

"Discount? I think not. This is a five-star establishment with a helipad on top. And you've got a suite, buddy boy. I arranged for early arrival. They were expecting you."

"So what? It's a hotel. I'll be there." He'd been too anxious to see Tess to check in at the hotel. As soon as he'd picked up his rental, he'd gone directly to her office. "Nice job on the rental. I like a Mercedes."

"I promise not to tell anybody about your champagne taste. It's not good for your tough guy image."

He heard the smirk in her voice and imagined her pushing her glasses up on her nose. Amelia was more than a receptionist or office assistant. In her unassuming but caustic way, she ran things at CSaI.

"Make travel arrangements," he said. "I want everybody up here."

"Not Nick Cavanaugh. He needs to be with Grace while her son is recovering from the bone marrow operation."

"Cavanaugh should stay, of course. Family comes first." More than ever before, he felt the truth of that statement.

"And I'm not scheduling anything until you tell me what's going on."

Nolan glanced toward the closed door to the bathroom. Though he was certain no one could hear him, he lowered his voice. "Our intel from Jessop is confirmed. Something's going down, and Bart is in the middle of it. I need man power."

"O-o-o-kay." She drawled the word. "It sounds like you're getting ready to storm the castle. How can I help?"

"We need to locate Victor Bellows or Wes Bradley or whatever he's calling himself." He remembered something Tess had said about the father-son relationship. "We need research on Victor's background, his childhood and teen years. Who were his friends? His teachers? His doctors? Who influenced his life? I want to know why he and Bart were estranged."

"I'm on it," she assured him. "In the meantime, I know exactly where you should start."

"Why am I not surprised?" Amelia had an uncanny knack for anticipating what they needed. He wasn't sure if she was psychic or just so much smarter than everybody else that she was mentally two steps ahead.

"Lila Lockhart and Bart were good friends when Victor was growing up. I'll bet she can tell you a lot. And she'll be arriving at Pierpont House tomorrow."

"Good call. Thanks, Amelia."

He disconnected the call. Once he had the rest of the CSaI team operating at full speed, Nolan would be free to do the most important job of all—protecting Tess and Joey.

ON THE DRIVE back to her office, Tess sorted through the notes she'd taken at the Zamir house. Every little detail—from the calligraphy on the place cards to the fresh basil for the pesto—had to be exactly right. If she organized properly now, she could set aside these preparations until after the Smithsonian event that would be occupying all her time for the next four days.

"It's a good thing I have my Christmas shopping done," she said. "The only trick now is to keep Joey from finding his presents."

"My mom used to wrap our presents and keep them locked in the trunk of her car," Nolan said. "Worked pretty well."

She remembered Joe telling her exactly the same story. So many little things about Nolan reminded her of him. "My mom wasn't that tricky."

"Did you find the presents?"

"Sometimes." During the holiday season, she missed her family. "This is the second year in a row that Joey and I won't be going to Chicago to share Christmas with my mom. Last year, the weather was too awful and the airport was closed. And there's no way I can leave this year. Not with Governor Lockhart's event."

"Do you have any other family nearby?"

"We're scattered all over the place," she said. "How about you? Do you stay in touch with your family?"

"Bart is the closest thing to family in my life."

Even if she disregarded his physical scars, Tess would have guessed that Nolan had suffered a lot. Sure, he was tough and more masculine than any man had a right to be. But there was also an aura of sadness and abandonment.

She asked, "Are you staying at the Pierpont House with Governor Lockhart's entourage?"

"I'm in a hotel near the Smithsonian."

Which probably meant he'd be alone tonight. Tess was struck by an impulse. *I want to ask him to come over for dinner.*

That idea was completely out of character. She seldom went on dates, and she never ever made the first move. Not that she thought there was anything improper about a woman asking a man out. It just never occurred to her.

Being a single mom and running a business took up all her energy. Her days were packed full from the moment she got out of bed until she collapsed at the end of the day. She didn't have time.

Tess inhaled a breath and looked out the window at cloudy skies. Time wasn't the issue, not really. She used to throw together last-minute dinner parties at the drop of a hat. When she and Joe first moved into their house, he was always bringing home other marines on leave with nowhere else to go. They'd done a lot of entertaining.

Her life was different now. Less spontaneous. More responsible. Oh my God, that was pathetic. She was hiding from a social life and turning into a hermit. She might as well hang out a "Closed" sign. *I'm going to ask him.* The worst that could happen was he'd say no.

She screwed up her courage. "If you're not doing anything else tonight, I'd like for you to come to my house for dinner. Nothing fancy, but I'm a pretty good cook."

"I'd be delighted," he said. "I'll bring wine."

She was so happy that she nearly clapped her hands. Nolan was only one person, but this would be a party. Unlike all the events she planned for other people, this was *her* party. She'd be the guest of honor. Actually, he was the guest. But she intended to enjoy every minute.

Why on earth hadn't she done this before? It was such a simple thing to invite someone to share a meal, but she'd never had the impulse until now...until she met Nolan.

He was the reason she'd opened up. Being with him inspired her and made her want to have fun.

"Red wine," she said.

"Shiraz?"

"Perfect."

She couldn't wait.

Chapter Six

At a quarter to six, Tess's phone rang. Her first thought was that it must be Nolan, calling to cancel. All afternoon, she'd been thinking about this dinner, elevating her level of excitement to a ridiculous high.

She'd gone back and forth a dozen times on the menu. A fabulous gourmet meal—like filet mignon or coq au vin—made it seem like she was trying too hard. But she couldn't just throw down a couple of burgers. In the end, there hadn't been time to visit the butcher or the fresh herb shop. She decided to keep it simple with two varieties of homemade pizza—one traditional and the other with a white pesto sauce.

Her cell phone kept ringing.

If Nolan couldn't come, she'd take it as a sign that she was getting her expectations too high. Joey dashed into the kitchen from the living room. "Mommy, answer your phone."

"I will." Ignoring bad news didn't make it go away. She grabbed her cell phone off the granite countertop and answered.

"Hi, it's Stacy." The governor's aide sounded rushed but happy. "How did it go with getting the blueprints?"

Though the meeting with Omar happened only this morning, it felt like ages ago. "According to Nolan's contact, the blueprints can't leave the Smithsonian, but they will be available to us."

"Very good. And now I have another problem."

Tess wasn't surprised. Only three days out from the event, there were bound to be issues and last-minute changes. Dealing with chaos was part of an event planner's job. "What's up?"

"Lila will be arriving early tomorrow, and she wants to see you at ten o'clock to talk about the menu. She'd like for you to come here to Pierpont House."

Tess looked over at Joey, who had climbed onto a stool at the serving counter and was reaching for one of the cream-filled chocolate cupcakes she'd made for dessert. Before she could stop him, he'd stolen a fingerful of dark chocolate icing and hopped down from the stool.

Into the phone, she said, "Could the governor reschedule our meeting for early afternoon?"

"I can check, but I'm not hopeful. Her day is packed. What do you have going on in the morning?"

If Stacy hadn't been the mother of a little boy herself, Tess never would have mentioned her problem. "It's babysitting. My son's regular day care provider is going out of town for Christmas, and I was planning to take Joey with me all day tomorrow."

"Bring him over here," Stacy said. "Zachary would love to have a buddy. And there are twin girls, four years old, coming on the plane with Lila."

"Twins?"

"I'm blaming Nolan. He decided to call in more guys from CSaI for security. One of them just got married to a close family friend, Lindsay Kemp. She's the mommy, and Lila insisted that she come with her new husband for Christmas Eve."

The Lockhart family and their large entourage of close

friends were a complicated bunch. Tess prided herself on being able to remember names and relationships for her clients, but she was beginning to feel like she needed a scorecard. "Lindsay Kemp, and she's a family friend."

"Right. And she's with Wade Coltrane. Her girls are Lacey and Lyric. They're adorable but a little overwhelming for Zachary. When he's around the twins, he retreats to a quiet corner and talks to his Matchbox cars. He'll be happy to have another boy to play with."

That was enough for Tess to agree. "I'll be there at ten, and I'll bring Joey."

As soon as she hung up, she went into the living room, where Joey had scattered pieces of his construction set across the coffee table. He liked to build skyscrapers, and she could easily imagine him growing up to be an architect. On the other hand, he took great pleasure in knocking down his creations, which probably pointed more toward a career in demolition.

Despite his career aspirations, Joey's most pronounced trait was his friendly, outgoing manner. His father had been the same way. Everybody was his friend. He never met a stranger.

When her son looked up, she noticed the telltale smudge of chocolate at the corner of his mouth. But she didn't reprimand him. A nibble before dinner wouldn't hurt.

She squatted beside him and wiped away the chocolate with her thumb. "Guess what you're doing tomorrow."

"Coming to work with you." He pointed at her.

"We'll have fun," she said with hopeful determination. "You're going to meet three new friends. There's a boy named Zachary and twin girls."

"Girls are dumb."

"Hey, I'm a girl."

"No, you're a mommy."

In a way, he was right. Her femininity was often eclipsed by her role as a mom. Nobody really cared what Joey's mom looked like as long as she got him to soccer practice on time. Except for work, she didn't fuss with her makeup or fixing her hair.

Tonight was different. When she'd gotten home, she'd showered, washed her hair and blow-dried it into a chic, smooth sweep to her shoulders. She'd abandoned her business suit for a pale blue cashmere sweater that brought out the blue of her eyes. Her favorite jeans did an amazing job of making her butt look perky. If she and Nolan had been dining alone, she would have gone all out with plunging necklines and high slits. But sultry didn't go well with pizza.

Joey bounced to his feet. "I'm hungry."

"Our guest will be here any minute." With her fingers, she combed his floppy brown hair out of his eyes. "I told you his name. Do you remember?"

"Mr. Law," Joey said. "And he was a marine. Like Daddy."

"You got it."

She'd talked with her son about Nolan's scars. Joey knew it was rude to criticize another person's appearance, but he was still prone to blurting out whatever crossed his mind. There wasn't much she could do—short of muzzling him—that would keep him quiet. She hoped her son wouldn't offend Nolan.

"Mommy, does Mr. Law have a gun?"

"Maybe." She knew that Nolan had been wearing a shoulder holster today, an occupational necessity for a man who worked security. Very likely, he'd be armed.

"When do we eat?"

"Very soon." Both pizzas were prepped and ready to go into the preheated oven.

The doorbell buzzed, and Joey ran toward it. As she followed, her heart raced with anticipation. She was slightly breathless, and the reaction annoyed her. This was only a casual dinner, not a command performance.

She pulled open the door. At this time of year, it was dark by six o'clock, and Nolan had exchanged his sunglasses for a pair of black horn-rimmed spectacles. Tall and broad-shouldered, he filled the doorframe. In one hand, he held a wine bottle. In the other was a bouquet of long-stemmed white and red roses.

"The flowers are lovely," she said, taking them from him.

Joey's head tilted back as he looked up at their guest. Her son held out his hand. "Nice to meet you, Mr. Law."

Nolan bent his knees and dropped to Joey's level to shake hands. A muscle in Nolan's jaw twitched. He looked pale. Maybe he wasn't well. His voice was huskier than usual when he said, "Nice to meet you, Joey."

"Can I ask you a question, Mr. Law?"

"Sure."

"Do you have a dog?"

"Not anymore," Nolan said. "But there's a border collie next door to where I live. He likes to play fetch."

"My mommy says I can't have a dog, but I asked Santa Claus, anyway. I want a Great Dane. I can ride him like a horse."

"Tell you what," Nolan said, "if you come and visit me in Texas, you can ride a real horse, like a cowboy."

Joey's eyes were huge as he looked up at her. "We gotta go to Texas."

"Any time," Nolan said as he stood.

She sought his gaze. Those vintage horn-rimmed glasses should have made him look like a nerd but they had the opposite effect. He was beyond rugged. Though she'd only known him for a few hours, his gray eyes were familiar. The only other time she'd felt this way about a man was when she met Joe.

She looked down at the long-stemmed roses. "I'll put these in water. I have the perfect vase for them."

He nodded as though he already knew about the tall, fluted crystal vase she'd received years ago as a wedding present.

Standing between them, Joey bleated, "Hungry. When do we eat?"

"Soon. Nolan, would you bring the wine?" She pivoted and went toward the kitchen. "I'm afraid we have to skip the appetizers. If I put out antipasto, Joey will be full before the main course."

In the kitchen, he placed the wine bottle on the counter. "I like what you've done in here."

"A couple of years ago, I went for a complete remodel." She'd changed out the worn cabinetry for dark oak, added black granite countertops, new appliances and knocked out the wall between kitchen and living room to make a breakfast counter. "I tried to stay with the original character of the house, but everything needed to be updated."

He rubbed his hands together. "Can I help with anything?"

"I'm sure you'd like to take off your jacket. Joey can show you where to hang it."

Joey waved him out of the kitchen. "Over here."

As she watched across the counter, Nolan followed her son into the living room where Joey showed off the Christmas tree they'd decorated. A pang of longing twisted in her stomach. Having a man around the house would be good for Joey. Not that he needed a role model to show him how to be masculine. In spite of spending most of his time with her as she cooked and planned fancy events, Joey was all boy.

He fired off a half-dozen questions about the horses in Texas. Were they big? Did they run faster than cars? Was there a school for horses?

Nolan answered patiently and with a sense of humor. He wasn't the least bit condescending with her son and seemed to be actually interested in Joey's running commentary. Somehow, she wasn't surprised that he was good with kids.

Joey said, "You don't look like a cowboy."

"I left my cowboy hat back at the ranch." The only hint of Texas was a pair of jeans that hugged him in all the right places. On top, Nolan wore a crewneck navy sweater. He dug into his pocket. "I do have this."

In his hand, he held a tin badge shaped in a five-pointed star with "Sheriff" written in bold script.

"Are you a sheriff?"

"No, but I like to catch bad guys."

"Me, too," Joey said.

"This badge is for you. Can I pin it on your shirt?"

Joey puffed out his skinny chest as Nolan fastened the badge to his shirt. The boy raced into the kitchen. "Look, Mommy. I'm a sheriff."

"Great." She really hoped Nolan wouldn't pull out his gun for show-and-tell. "We'll be ready to eat in fifteen minutes."

"Mommy, you cook." Joey grasped Nolan's hand and pulled him into the living room. "You come with me."

She slipped the two pizzas into the oven and returned to the counter to whip up a dressing for the green salad. This was exactly the sort of homey scene she'd imagined when she knocked out the wall between the kitchen and living room. She was in the kitchen, the heart of the house. And her men were in the living room. *Her men?* What was she thinking? She had no such claim on Nolan Law.

After Joey showed him the skyscraper he was building, the boy studied his new friend and frowned. "Mommy said I shouldn't ask about what happened to your face."

Tess cringed inside.

Calmly, Nolan replied, "You're curious, right?"

"Yeah."

Drying her hands on a dishtowel, she bustled into the living room, hoping to create a distraction. "Nolan, I could use your help in the kitchen. The wine bottle needs—"

He raised a hand. "It's okay, Tess."

WHEN PEOPLE ASKED about his injuries, Nolan usually put them off with a short reply. The question didn't bear asking. Obviously, he'd been injured and had gone through a lot of surgery. The gory details were nobody else's business.

But Joey and Tess deserved to hear the whole story. They didn't know it yet, but his injuries had impacted their lives. He wanted them to understand.

"Here's the thing, Joey." He settled back against the sofa. "I used to be in the Marine Corps."

"Like my daddy."

"That's right."

Though his voice stayed calm, he was yelling inside. *It's me. Joey, I'm your dad. Me!*

When he'd walked through the door and had seen this kid, Nolan had been so overwhelmed that he almost keeled over. The bond between them was stronger and more powerful than anything he'd felt before. The love was instantaneous—the love and the regret. How the hell could he have missed out on four-and-a-half years of his son's life?

"I was stationed in Afghanistan," he said. "Do you know where that is?"

"Very far," Joey said. "And there's a war."

"A long, hard-fought war. My squad was five guys. We were doing recon. That's short for reconnaissance, and it means we were looking around to see what kind of danger might be waiting for the rest of our platoon."

"What's a platoon?"

"More guys. Maybe thirty or forty."

"Do you have lots of guns and stuff?"

"A lot," he said. "A fully-equipped marine with protective gear, weaponry, water and food can be hauling eighty or even a hundred pounds of stuff. But my squad was traveling light and fast. It was night when we entered the village."

Far away from any major population center, there were only dirt roads through the desolate landscape. "The villages in Afghanistan aren't like any town you've ever seen. The houses are mud bricks and rough wood frames. There's no electricity. Just lanterns and battery-powered lights. We moved silently as shadows."

Joey climbed up onto the sofa beside him and sat on his heels. This moment was something Nolan had dreamed about—sitting here in the house he and Tess had purchased after they were married, telling a story to his son.

He glanced over at her. Instead of returning to the kitchen, she'd stayed and perched on the arm of an overstuffed chair they'd bought together. Was she feeling any of this intensity? Did she know him? Did she suspect?

"Our mission," he said, "was to locate a dangerous man who was known to be in the area."

"Did you find him?" Joey asked.

"Yes, we found him."

He hadn't known at the time that locating Greenaway

would irreparably change his life. Greenaway was more than an arms dealer who dealt in the opium trade. He was a death merchant who not only provided weapons but strategized to promote his wares, prolong the conflict and kill soldiers and civilians.

Bart had been on Greenaway's trail for years and considered him to be his nemesis. If Nolan could have changed the past, he never would have approached that desolate village.

"What happened next?" Joey asked.

"We went toward a house where we could see light even though the curtains were closed. The walls were very thick—made of stones plastered over with dirt—but there were spaces around the windows. We stayed hidden and listened."

Greenaway had been meeting with two warlords, explaining his plan for an exchange of weapons for opium. Though the American blended in with the others, mimicking their garb and covering half his face with a scarf, he spoke Pashto with an undeniable Texan accent.

Instead of charging through the door, Nolan listened intently. These details were important. If he could get the info to the right people, he could disrupt a major distribution network.

"When we'd heard enough, we decided to get out of there. We could stop a bad thing from happening if we told the right people what we'd learned."

Joey bobbed his head. "Silent as shadows, you went away."

"But we didn't make it to safety."

Chapter Seven

From the kitchen, Nolan heard the buzz of a timer. In a way, the interruption was perfect timing. The rest of his story got more painful.

Tess jumped to her feet and said, "The pizzas are done."

"Not now, Mommy." Joey threw both hands in the air. "Mr. Law is telling a story."

"But, Joey, I thought you were starving."

A bemused grin curved her soft pink lips as she glanced in Nolan's direction. The more he was with her, the more beautiful she became. He'd gotten over the initial shock of seeing her and was noticing details. Her silky black hair was longer and straighter. She'd lost weight, and her cheekbones were more pronounced. When she smiled, he saw faint crinkles at the outer edges of her blue eyes.

Five years ago, she'd told him that lines on a woman's face were crinkles, not wrinkles. Whatever she called them, they were prettier than makeup. The crinkles made her real. For years, he'd been staring at her photograph. Reality was a hell of a lot better.

She was running the show, giving the orders. "Please continue, Nolan. I can hear you from the kitchen."

"Yeah," Joey said. "Did you get the bad guy?"

"We made it out of the village. The moon and starlight

were enough for us to see where we were going. Then the firefight started and we were pinned down."

"They had fire?" Joey asked.

"A firefight is what you call it when guys are firing at each other," he explained. "We radioed for help, but our platoon was miles away and we were outnumbered."

"Were you scared?"

"You bet I was." He looked into his son's eyes, imparting the kind of wisdom that fathers were supposed to say. "No matter what anybody tells you, it's okay to be scared when you're in danger."

"Then what?"

These were details that couldn't be told. Greenaway had called out to them. Speaking in English, he demanded to know what they'd heard. Nolan still remembered the voice. Harsh and cold as the Afghan night, the words echoed inside his skull. If they told anyone about Greenaway's plans, he would take his revenge on them and their families. Their wives and children would suffer tortures beyond comprehension. Their loved ones would beg for death.

Nolan and the four other marines with him remained silent. Though Greenaway couldn't possibly know their identities, his threats rang true. According to the CIA, his influence extended beyond the war zone.

"Our backup troops arrived in three units. One of my men was injured, but we escaped and were on our way back to rejoin our platoon."

None of the men who were with Nolan spoke Pashto. They had overheard the same conversation, but it sounded like gibberish to them. He was the only one who knew the details of Greenaway's operation, and he needed to get that information to someone who could use it. At the same time, he needed to be covert. He wouldn't do anything that would put Tess in danger. He contacted the CIA in Kandahar.

"The next morning, my squad and a couple of other guys were on our way to a city."

"Wait a minute," Joey interrupted. "Did the bad guys get away?"

"I'm afraid so."

"That's not how it's supposed to turn out. Bad guys get caught. Good guys win."

"Who's telling this story? You or me?"

Joey wiggled around beside him. "You still didn't say how you got hurt."

"That comes next." He looked over his shoulder toward the dining area where Tess was pouring Shiraz into glasses with stems that had been a wedding present. "Looks like your mom is just about ready for dinner."

She came to the front room. "I'm listening."

As his wife and his son looked at him with total acceptance, he almost forgot his scars—an irony. The whole point of his story was to explain what had happened to his face.

"On our way to a city called Kandahar, our vehicle ran over a bomb." Explaining the concept of an IED to Joey was too complicated. "That's how I got injured. If I hadn't been wearing my helmet and protective armor, I would have been dead for sure. As it was, I had broken bones in my left arm and leg, internal damage and serious burns. My throat was nearly crushed. A lot of the bones in my face were shattered."

"Which ones?" Joey asked.

"Across my brow. My jaw. A cheekbone. My nose."

After the IED, his memories had been incoherent. He'd thought he was dead, had never expected to survive. He couldn't see, but he'd heard a voice, Greenaway's voice, coming from above him. Greenaway spoke his name. *Joe Donovan.* He hadn't been able to move, couldn't defend himself. *Joe Donovan, it's good that you're dead. I don't have to kill you. Or your pregnant wife.*

"The next thing I remember is being in a field hospital. They didn't think I was going to make it."

For a moment, he flashed back in time.

A CIA agent was at his side, asking about Greenaway. Though it was nearly impossible to speak, Nolan forced the words through his bloody lips.

His throat was raw. Every breath was a struggle. This was his dying declaration. Greenaway already thought he was dead. Tess wouldn't be in danger. The last agonizing words he uttered were meant for her, his dearest love.

After that, things got weird. He heard the CIA agent tell the medic that he was gone. They pulled a sheet over his face and declared him dead. Along with two other injured men, he was evacuated in a chopper.

He wanted to tell somebody that he was still alive, but he couldn't move, couldn't feel a damn thing.

Shaking off the memory, he looked at Joey and shrugged. "That's about it. At a hospital in Switzerland, I met Bart Bellows for the first time."

"I know Bart," Joey said.

Tess moved closer, taking more of an interest. "Was that before or after Bart retired?"

"A guy like Bart never retires. He just changes focus. I became his personal reclamation project, which was lucky for me. Bart arranged for some of the best specialists in the world to put me back together."

"How did they fix you?" Joey asked.

"With a lot of physical therapy. They reinforced the bone in my leg with metal." He stretched his left leg out in front of him. The doctors hadn't expected him to walk again, but he'd worked hard to prove them wrong. "This leg is almost bionic. You know, like a robot."

"Cool."

"They rebuilt the bones in my face and slapped on some new skin. For a while, I looked like Mr. Potato Head with pieces missing."

Joey patted his scarred cheek, and the touch of his son's hand was magic. Nolan felt his jaw stretch into a smile of purest joy. Life was worth living again.

Maybe, someday, he could even return to his identity as Joe Donovan. But not yet. Not while Greenaway was still a threat.

As they went to the dinner table, Tess leaned close to him. "Thanks for talking to Joey."

"I wish I'd had a better story. You know, something about me going Rambo and wiping out a thousand bad guys."

"Your version is better. I don't want my son to think war is some kind of fun video game."

"You're right about that."

She casually touched his arm, and he felt healed. Between her and Joey, he'd experienced more affectionate contact in the past fifteen minutes than he had in the past five years.

Quietly, she said, "I didn't know you were so close to Bart. I think of him as my guardian angel, and I guess he was protecting you, too."

Bart Bellows protected all of them, more than she knew. To compensate Nolan for giving the CIA enough intelligence to nearly destroy Greenaway's lethal distribution system, Bart used his contacts to make sure Joe Donovan appeared to be dead. He'd arranged the monthly payments Tess received, supposedly from the Veterans Administration and a life insurance policy. And he'd violated myriad regulations and ordinances by arranging for an empty coffin to be buried at Arlington under Joe Donovan's headstone.

The ruse seemed to have worked. Greenaway believed that Joe Donovan died before he could pass on the information he'd overheard. He blamed someone else for the problems the CIA had caused him.

When Nolan had recovered enough to make decisions for himself, he wanted to go back to Tess. He and Bart had explored all the options from entering a witness protection program to moving into an armed fortress. No matter what he did, Tess and Joey would be in mortal danger—targets for Greenaway's brutal vengeance.

This afternoon when Nolan discovered that the Zamirs were still keeping an eye on Tess, his fears had been confirmed. Greenaway hadn't forgotten about Joe Donovan. Nolan knew he'd done the right thing by staying away.

But would Tess see it the same way? His fake death had caused her heartache. Would she understand that he'd stayed away because he had no other choice?

Sitting at the head of the table with Joey on his left and Tess on his right, he wanted to make the announcement. The words crawled up his throat. He wanted to end the separation that had lasted for five long, painful years. Desperately, he wanted his family back. If he couldn't be with them, he might as well put a bullet in his head and finish the job Greenaway had started in Afghanistan.

He took a bite of the traditional pizza. The familiar flavor of her homemade tomato sauce sparked old memories. She hadn't changed the combination of savory spices.

"This sauce is amazing," he said.

"The recipe is an old standby," she said. "I like to make up a big batch and use it throughout the week on spaghetti and lasagna."

He remembered. "I'll bet it smells great when it's cooking."

"Try the white pizza," she said. "The sauce is a combination of pesto and parmesan over toppings of shredded chicken and veggies."

"It's cheesy," Joey said as he swallowed. "My mom is the best cook in the world."

"What's your favorite dish?" Nolan asked.

Joey looked up at the ceiling as he considered, and then he grinned. "Cupcakes. I can eat a hundred cupcakes."

"Yeah?" Nolan grinned back at him. "Do you know how many a hundred is?"

"Sure."

Joey started counting, losing interest somewhere in the fifties. Then he talked about adding and reading and all the things he was learning in day care. Next year, he'd be in kindergarten.

They settled into what he supposed was a normal conversation—telling anecdotes, exchanging smiles and even occasionally laughing. Nolan tried to settle himself into this pleasant version of life. It was surreal.

He questioned how he could be sitting at the dining table in the house that he and Tess had shared while, at the same time, being a stranger. Though he had helped her choose the plates and the silverware, he couldn't help commenting on the blue and yellow pattern so he could hear her say that those were such cheerful colors. He knew Tess and Joey were his family, but they had no idea.

While Tess put Joey to bed, Nolan checked out the Christmas tree. He remembered the ornaments from her family. There were no heirlooms from him; both his parents were dead.

He went to the accent wall in the living room. He remembered the day they had painted. She hadn't changed the color. It was still a light chocolate brown. The arrangement of photographs above the rolltop desk she'd inherited from her grandma was the same as when he'd lived here with Tess, including a casual picture of both of them on vacation in the Bahamas standing next to a palm tree. Damn, they'd been a good-looking couple. When he'd helped her hang these pictures, he'd been careless and had damaged the plaster. Was it still there?

He took down a sepia photo of Tess's grandparents on their wedding day. There was the crack. He ran his fingers over the wall.

"What are you doing, Nolan?"

Tess had returned from the bedroom. She stood in the hallway, watching him.

"This picture," he said, "was off center. If you'd like, I could fix that wall for you."

Though she still looked confused, she shook her head. "We have more important things to worry about."

He replaced the photo. "Such as?"

"Bart."

She went into the living room, sat on the sofa and picked up her wineglass. Tess had never been much of a drinker; she had one glass with dinner and one after. Even so, he noticed a flush in her cheeks as she continued, "When you were talking about Bart, I remembered what a truly good man he is. It just doesn't make sense that he'd have such terrible problems with his son."

Nolan could damn sure point to himself as an example of a man who was a decent human being and a lousy father. "There must have been circumstances."

"I'm supposed to meet with Governor Lockhart tomorrow morning," she said. "I know she's old friends with Bart. Is there any chance that she'd know something about his son?"

"We've talked to her." He sat on the sofa beside Tess, close enough to feel the warmth radiating from her body and to catch a whiff of her unique fragrance. "Lila doesn't have a clue about Victor's whereabouts."

"I was thinking that there might be a clue in the past," she said. "Maybe she can tell us about when Victor was a child. Some patterns develop early."

And Lila Lockhart might be more inclined to talk about those patterns with another woman. "I'll be there, too. I can make sure you have time to talk to her."

"I know she's a busy woman, but this is about Bart."

Reaching for his wineglass on the coffee table, his shoulder brushed hers. He clinked the rim of his glass against hers. "Thank you for inviting me for dinner."

"I'm glad you could come." Her wistful smile touched him. "You were terrific with Joey."

"He's a good kid."

And he was in bed. Now was adult time. His gaze linked with hers. Her blue eyes were soft and misty. She lowered her lids, leaned a bit closer to him.

Bracing himself for the sensation of her lips joining with his, he anticipated her kiss. The air vibrated with possibility. His heartbeat was a sledgehammer inside his chest.

She pulled back. "Nolan, there's something I have to say."

"Okay."

His guard went up. Expecting a kiss on their first date might be too much to hope for. Even if she didn't consciously know who he was, he was damn sure that she felt the same pull that he did, the same magnetism. They had been part of each other.

She looked down into her wineglass. Her sooty lashes formed graceful crescents above her cheeks. "I've been a widow for five years, and I haven't dated much. I need to go slow."

"I understand."

"And I might never be able to…have a relationship with another man. The truth is…" She looked up at him. "I still love my husband."

And I love you, my darling Tess. With all my heart.

Chapter Eight

At ten o'clock the next morning, Tess stood at a bay window in a sitting room at the front of Pierpont House. She looked out at a garden area that was probably gorgeous in the springtime. Even now, in the dead of winter, the grounds were attractive with a light snow tracing the rose bushes and the bare branches of trees.

Leaving the window, she sat in a Federal-style chair with gold-and-black upholstery and mahogany arms. As she sipped perfectly brewed coffee from a delicate china cup, she counted the ways that she'd violated proper business procedures.

Number one: There wasn't time this morning to stop at the office to brief Trudy on the day's events, and Tess was carrying all the information about the Zamir dinner in her briefcase.

Number two: She'd brought Joey along with her to an appointment. After Stacy met her in the foyer, they'd trekked through the mansion to a cheerful playroom near the kitchen where the preschool twin girls and Stacy's autistic son were being watched by the twins' mother and her new husband. Joey didn't mind being dropped off; he loved playing with new friends.

Number three: Like it or not, she was involved with

Nolan. Close personal relationships with clients and their staff counted as a huge breach in professional behavior.

Even worse, Tess was about to break another rule. She intended to step outside her role as event planner and ask the governor personal questions about Bart's son. What was she thinking? It was vital to make a good impression with Lila Lockhart. If Tess performed well on this event, her career could really take off.

The smart thing would be to keep her mouth shut and do her job to the best of her ability. But Lila might have the answers. Saving Bart was more important than anything else.

She crossed and uncrossed her legs. In spite of the chilly weather, she'd worn a gray suit with a tulip skirt and black pumps. At least she was dressed like a career woman.

When the door opened, she placed her cup onto the saucer and set it on the wood-inlay coffee table. She popped to her feet, straightened her spine and fixed a polite smile on her lips.

It was Nolan. The sight of him sent a rush of excitement through her. He closed the door behind him and sauntered toward her. "At ease, soldier."

"Are you saying that I look tense?"

"You look great. Nice necklace."

"Thanks." The old-fashioned silver locket engraved with her initials had been a gift from Joe.

He took a seat in the matching chair opposite her. His muscular body seemed too big for the spindly-legged antique. "I wanted to be here when you talked to Lila about Bart. I'm not going to say much, but I'm a good listener."

"You might have to sit through another in-depth discussion of menus and table arrangements," she warned him.

"I can handle it."

His easy grin surprised her. All day yesterday, he'd barely cracked a smile. Last night, he'd loosened up over dinner, and now he seemed positively relaxed.

His upbeat attitude relieved her. After she'd declared her undying love for Joe, she'd expected Nolan to back away from her so fast that he tripped over his own feet. Instead, he seemed even warmer toward her. Or was he? The man was hard to read, not just because of the ever-present dark glasses and the strong, silent attitude. There was something intriguing about him, something that made her curious, something special.

Her gaze calibrated the breadth of his shoulders. He was wearing the same navy crewneck sweater as last night. The button-down collar of his shirt and cuffs were white, just like last night. He must be one of those guys who found an acceptable outfit and wore it like a uniform.

"I met Wade Coltrane," she said. The twins' father had welcomed Joey into the playroom with open arms. "He's more of a cowboy than you."

"Wade grew up in Freedom, Texas."

"Have the other men from CSaI arrived?"

"The gang's all here. Coltrane will be overseeing security here at the house. Not a difficult assignment. A lot of high-risk individuals stay at Pierpont House, so the place comes with a security contingent. It's a fortress."

"I know." Joey had been thrilled when they pulled up at the gate, and he saw the armed guard. "They checked my credentials before they'd let me inside."

"There's bulletproof glass in the windows and security cameras watching the perimeter. Even a panic room where everybody can hide in case of assault."

There had been a number of threats on the governor and her family. "I thought the danger to the Lockharts had passed. Are all these precautions necessary?"

"Being prepared is better than the alternative."

Governor Lockhart swept into the room like a petite blond cyclone with Stacy following in her wake. The governor's energy was amazing, even more so because she'd had surgery, donating bone marrow to her grandson, less than a month ago. Before the door closed, she was already talking. "Thanks for coming over on short notice, Tess. I just had a few teensy-weensy details that I wanted to make sure you were aware of."

In a choreographed greeting, she shook Tess's hand and turned to Nolan. When she reached up to hug him, her sharp blue eyes stared into his sunglasses. "Any news on Bart?"

"Actually, Lila, we were hoping you might help us out on our investigation."

"We?" She glanced back and forth between them. "I didn't know you two were acquainted."

Tess spoke up, "Our connection is Bart. Over the years, he's been a good friend to both me and Nolan. More than a friend, actually. If it wasn't for Bart, I don't know how I would have survived my husband's death."

"Bart Bellows is a good man to lean on." She sank onto the sofa, crossed her legs and gave Stacy a nod. "Would you please adjust my schedule? I'm going to take as long as needed with this conversation."

"Absolutely," Stacy said as she exited.

Tess liked the no-nonsense way the governor did business. "I appreciate it, ma'am."

"Call me Lila. I insist. Now, how can I help?"

"We're looking for anything you can remember about Bart's son," Tess said. "It's likely that Victor is responsible for taking his father hostage, and they're probably in this area. Nolan tells me there's nothing in the military or civilian databases that gives any kind of clue as to where

Victor might be or why he'd do this to his father. Your personal recollections might provide a lead."

"I've only met Victor a couple of times," Lila said.

"Could you tell me about the first time?" Tess asked. "Anything you can remember."

"It was over twenty years ago, just after Bart's wife passed away. I was a young mother. Oh my, that was so very long ago." Absentmindedly, she played with her diamond cross necklace. "Bart thought it might be good for his son to experience the wide-open spaces at the ranch."

"Was he having problems with Victor?"

"He was a difficult kid. Brooding and silent, but when he started talking, he wouldn't stop. My daughter was a tiny pixie with bright blond hair. You couldn't help loving little Bailey, but Victor got really mad at her when she touched his things. He shouted at her, told her she was a bad girl."

"Did Bart discipline him?" Tess asked.

"You bet. Bart wouldn't stand for rude behavior. Victor's nanny wasn't so strict."

Tess went fishing for a lead. "Do you remember the name of the nanny?"

"Her first name was Roxanne. I remember because of the Sting song by that name. *Roxanne.* She was a hot little number, a redhead. I had the impression that she was more interested in becoming Bart's second wife than in taking care of his son. I don't think Victor liked her."

"Why?"

"He played tricks on her. When they went riding, he spooked her horse and she could have really been hurt."

"Roxanne's last name?"

"I don't know." Lila shook her head. "I remember feeling sorry for Victor. He was almost a teenager. That's a rough time for anybody. And he'd lost his mother."

There was something in her tone that made Tess think there was more to the story. "What about his relationship with Bart?"

"I love Bart," she said firmly. "He's a man of action. Tough, strong and a patriot to the core. But he's not the world's greatest dad. After his wife died, he threw himself into his CIA career and was gone for long periods of time. I was always grateful that my late husband put family first."

"I've noticed," Tess said, "that Bart isn't big on giving hugs. But I thought it was because of the wheelchair."

"Oh my no, he's never been a touchy-feely person, and he seemed extra reserved with his son. Once, I saw him put his arm around Victor's shoulder, and the boy cringed like he'd been hit. He didn't want to be touched."

"Do you think Victor was autistic?"

"I don't know about that," Lila said. "But I'm pretty sure that boy was traumatized when his mother died."

Tess was developing a mental image of Bart's son. As a preteen, he was sullen and angry. He missed his mom and resented his dad. Not a pretty picture, but not unusual.

Nothing Lila had said thus far explained Victor's violent criminal behavior. When he kidnapped Bart, he'd set an explosive at a day care center. He'd murdered Bart's driver. Nolan had told her that his military record showed acts of cruelty that would have resulted in a dishonorable discharge if he hadn't been presumed missing.

She asked, "Did Victor have problems in school?"

"He was smart as a whip but a terrible student. Bart ended up putting him in a boarding school, and that seemed to work well. Bart bragged that his boy spoke half a dozen languages and was headed for a career as a nuclear scientist, and then it fell apart."

"What happened?"

"I'm not sure of the details," Lila said. "In Victor's senior year, he and some of his pals got into a feud with some of the other boys. There were fights. And a building got burned down."

"Burned?" Nolan questioned. "Were explosives involved?"

"All I know is that five boys, including Victor, were expelled. That was when Bart pressured his son to join the army."

Tess looked to Nolan. "Do you know anything about that school?"

"It's in Bethesda, not far from here. Might be useful to visit there and locate some of Victor's old gang."

She knew that they were both thinking the same thing. Victor's penchant for explosives might have started young.

Lila snapped her fingers. "I remember something. Just after basic training, Bart came to the ranch with Victor. Long story short, he injured himself in the barn. Nothing serious, but I called the doctor to come to the ranch and stitch him up. Dr. Leigh is a very perceptive man."

"What did the doc have to say?" Tess asked.

"Plenty." Though they were the only people in the room, Lila lowered her voice. "He warned me to steer clear of Victor Bellows and to keep my kids away from him. Dr. Leigh said that Victor had a hair-trigger temper and couldn't be blamed for his actions."

"Couldn't be blamed?" That was an odd way of phrasing a warning. "What does that mean?"

"I'm not real sure," Lila admitted. "The doc wouldn't tell me anything else because it violated doctor-patient confidentiality. You know what I'm thinking? I should have discussed Victor's behavior with Bart, should have made more of an effort to tell him that there were real problems."

"Do you have Dr. Leigh's phone number?"

"Stacy can get it for you." She looked toward Nolan. "Was it Victor who almost blew up my daughter's day care center?"

He nodded. "I don't think he meant to kill anybody. He was using the bomb as a diversion so he could grab his father."

"All those babies were in danger," Lila said. "If I'd sat down with Bart and made him see that his son was violent, things might have been different."

"It's not your fault," Tess said quickly.

"I'm not blaming myself. Lord knows, I've got enough to repent." She exhaled a sigh. "That's just about all I can think of that might be useful. If anything else occurs to me, I'll let you know."

Nolan rose from his chair, came toward her and patted her shoulder. "Thanks, Lila. You gave us some leads to work on."

"You keep me posted." She turned to Tess. "Now, are we ready to talk about fruit cups and ice sculptures?"

"Of course."

The rapid change of topic threw Tess off guard. She juggled her laptop, purse and briefcase. As she lifted the briefcase onto the coffee table, the file folder containing the information on the Zamir dinner slipped out. The contents cascaded across the carpet.

"Oops." She dropped to her knees to gather her papers. Fortunately, she kept most of her data on her laptop. There wasn't all that much clutter, only a couple of seating charts, a guest list and calligraphy samples that might be used on invitations and place cards.

She reached for a scrap. Her elbow bumped the coffee table. Her dainty coffee cup skittered toward the edge. In a frantic grab, she caught the saucer before it spilled. "It's okay. I got it."

Damn, damn, damn. She'd gotten through the difficult talk with Lila unscathed. They'd even bonded. Now, Tess felt like a total klutz. Could she possibly be more unprofessional?

Nolan squatted beside her and helped her. He held a sheet of paper and stared at it. "What's this?"

She glanced at a list of names. Mrs. Zamir's penmanship was impeccable. "A guest list."

He pointed. "Do you know these people?"

"I've met some of them. This isn't the first time I've worked with the Zamirs."

Lila spoke up. "Do you know the Zamirs? That oldest daughter is a real beauty. A little wild, though."

Tess wasn't surprised that Lila knew them. Saudis and Texans shared a common interest in oil. "I've planned several events for Mrs. Zamir. I even found an importer for their chai tea that—"

"Tess." Nolan snapped her name. He held the guest list under her nose. "Do you know this man?"

She read the name and shook her head. "Greenaway? That doesn't sound familiar."

He bolted toward the door. "Don't leave. We need to talk."

Chapter Nine

Nolan held himself together until he'd stumbled into the corridor outside the sitting room and closed the door. A tidal wave of tension and fear crashed over him. He braced his back against the wall to keep his knees from buckling. Greenaway was close, so close that Tess knew his name. She was in danger. And Joey, too. If anything happened to them...

"Hey, man." Coltrane sauntered toward him. "You look like roadkill. Are you okay?"

"You should be watching the kids," he snapped. Security should be tighter. They should call in a battalion to protect their families.

"I needed a break," Coltrane said. "There's only so many tea parties that a man can take."

"It's not safe." Even though Pierpont House was a fortress of brick and bulletproof glass, they were under threat.

Coltrane tilted his head to the left and squinted into Nolan's eyes. "Something's up. Are you going tell me?"

Nolan fought his anxiety. His head throbbed. He rubbed the tips of his fingers against his temples as he willed himself to be calm. The situation called for cool, direct action. Panic would get him nowhere. "Do you remember the name Jessop mentioned? Greenaway?"

"A contact of Wes Bradley. Big-time distributor of

opium and illegal weapons in Afghanistan. What about him?"

"He's closing in," Nolan said. "He's been keeping an eye on Tess Donovan."

"The party planner? Joey's mom?" Coltrane was obviously surprised. "How does a nice lady like her get connected to an international sleazeball?"

"Through Bart. He's a close friend of hers." He caught his breath. "Bart referred Lila to Tess."

"And now she's in as much danger as the rest of us," Coltrane concluded. "She and Joey need to stay here where we can provide protection."

"Correct." He was grateful that Coltrane needed no further convincing. There wasn't time for explanations.

"What do we do next?"

"I'd like to mount a full-scale assault, but I can't risk losing Greenaway or calling attention to us." He recalled the heinous details of Greenaway's threats in Afghanistan. His small band of brothers in CSaI didn't have the man power or the influence to effectively pursue. "I'll turn my information over to Omar Harris at the CIA."

"We play it low-key but maintain high alert."

"Exactly." Nolan's headache faded to a dull thump. He was beginning to think more rationally. They were already on their way toward finding Victor, and he suspected from the conversation he'd overheard at the Zamirs' that Victor—using his Wes Bradley alias—was a part of this plot. "We focus on locating Victor. I got a couple of leads from Lila."

Coltrane bobbed his head in a quick nod. He was a dark, muscular, good-looking guy—as smart as he was handsome. "Tell me where to start."

"Victor had a nanny named Roxanne after his mom died. See if you can find her last name or the service she worked for. And he went to a boarding school in Bethesda."

"That's close to here."

"And I'm hoping some of his old school buddies might still live in this area. They had a gang that was responsible for burning down a building. Victor might have stayed in touch with one of his former friends."

"I'll contact Amelia back at the office. She's a genius when it comes to tracking down the impossible." Coltrane shook his head. "Burned down a building? Sounds like young Victor was a hell-raiser. How could Bart's kid turn out so bad?"

Nolan remembered Lila's comment about the doctor who said it wasn't really Victor's fault. Dr. Leigh was the lead he'd follow up on immediately. Prying confidential information from a doctor would be a whole lot easier than convincing Tess that she and Joey needed to stay at Pierpont House.

AFTER NOLAN GOT Dr. Leigh's phone number from Stacy, he found a quiet space in an office on the first floor to make the call. Through the window, he could see the side of the house where Tess's SUV was parked among all the other vehicles. If she tried to leave without talking to him, he'd know it.

He spotted one of the armed security guards keeping watch over the cars, vans and SUVs. Good. Lila chose to stay at Pierpont House because it was beautiful; CSaI approved because it was well-protected.

His cell phone came with a scrambler so his signal couldn't be traced via GPS or his conversation monitored. All the guys had the latest in technology thanks to Bart's connections and his wealth. Nolan was grateful for the stealth phone when he contacted Omar Harris, informing him about Greenaway and the Zamirs.

This part of the investigation was best left to the CIA. They had the connections and the authority. Nolan still feared the wrath of Greenaway. He wanted to keep a distance.

He left the window and sat behind a carved mahogany desk with a wall of leather-bound books behind him—a setting fit for an aristocrat. He longed for the plain surroundings of the CSaI offices. A simple life was all he wanted. In his mind, the house that he and Tess had bought to raise their family was just about perfect.

Whether or not he and Tess ended up as a couple, he needed to preserve that lifestyle for her and Joey. Failure was not an option. He had to make the right moves, and he wished Bart was here to advise him. They worked well together. Bart was like the football coach who came up with the game plan, and Nolan was the quarterback who executed logistics. Taking on both roles strained his brain.

He punched in the phone number for Dr. Gregory Leigh of Freedom, Texas. According to Stacy, the doctor was in his late sixties but still maintained a small practice for his longtime patients. He answered the phone himself. "Howdy, this is Dr. Leigh."

Nolan had been expecting the quiet tones of a gentle, gray-haired country doctor. Dr. Leigh sounded more like a booming Texan bull rider.

"My name is Nolan Law, and I was given your number by Lila Lockhart. I need to ask you a few questions about a patient you saw several years ago."

"I know you," the doctor said. "Y'all work with Bart Bellows at Corps Security and Investigations."

"Yes, sir."

"Are you the one who had extensive facial reconstruction? Someday, when you got time, I'd sure like to discuss those procedures."

Nolan couldn't refuse, not when he was about to ask a favor. "We can meet when I get back to Freedom. Right now, I'm in D.C. with the governor. She told me that you once treated Bart's son, Victor."

"Hell's bells, that was around twenty years ago, but I remember. I surely do. Victor Bellows was nineteen years old and just finished up basic training. I was thinking this kid might be deployed. Back then, y'all know, we were on the brink of the first Gulf War in Iraq."

"What can you tell me about Victor?"

"He had a cut on his forearm, the left forearm. And I stitched him up." There was a pause. "That's all I can say, Nolan. On account of patient confidentiality."

"I understand." Nolan had expected this objection. "You're a man of ethics—a man who does the right thing."

"Sure as hell am."

"I'm going to tell you the truth, Dr. Leigh. Then you can decide what's right." There wasn't time to subpoena his records or legally compel him to cooperate. "Victor has been living under an alias and has likely been involved in illegal activities in Afghanistan and Iraq. Our investigation points toward Victor as the person who set the explosion at the Cradles to Crayons Day Care Center and kidnapped his father."

"Good lord." The thunderous voice lowered. "Bart's driver was killed."

"Murdered," Nolan said. "We're trying to understand what motivates someone like Victor. Lila said you were a perceptive man. Is there anything you can tell me?"

"I'll help. It's the right thing. But you need to keep in mind that I'm a small-town doc, not a psychiatrist. I never did run physical or psychological tests on Victor. What I'm about to say is based purely on my impressions. You got that?"

"Yes, sir."

"When I went to the Twin Harts Ranch to treat Victor's injury, he didn't want me to touch him. Gave me a shove that knocked me backward, and that's quite a feat. I'm a big man. Two hundred and sixty pounds, six foot four. Anyhow, Victor had two long, nasty gashes on his arm, and he kept saying that he had the power to heal himself. Nothing could hurt him. He was invincible."

"Was he in pain?"

"Not so much that he'd be delusional. He was talking a mile a minute. Highly agitated and hostile. I finally got him to sit his butt down and let me put in a few stitches. He jumped to his feet. His eyes were ablaze. He stared right through me as he lifted his arm to his face and tore out the stitches with his teeth. I'll never forget it. Blood smeared all over his face, and he was laughing."

No wonder Leigh remembered the incident. "Did you call for help?"

"Have you ever seen a rattlesnake, coiled and ready to strike? Well, I have. I froze and watched and listened to the click of the rattles until the snake gave up and slithered away. That's how it was with Victor. I was fascinated."

"Why was he acting that way?"

"I wanted to believe he was a young soldier under stress. They run plenty of tests in the army. I couldn't believe they'd let somebody slip through who was suffering from a serious mental illness. But Victor was exhibiting extreme symptoms of what's now called bipolar disorder. I wouldn't call that a diagnosis. As I mentioned before, I'm no psychiatrist."

"What happened next?"

"Victor allowed me to work on his arm. He was arrogant as all hell and angry. I figured he was dangerous, and I warned Lila to keep her kids away from him. By the time I finished stitching him up, Victor was behaving normally."

"Did you talk to Bart?"

"I gave it a shot. Sometimes, a loved one is the last to see trouble coming. His father had no idea of what I was talking about. Y'all got to understand. Victor was extremely smart—clever enough to hide his symptoms from Bart or anybody else who stood in his way."

Nolan was aware that bipolar disorder was a chemical imbalance that responded well to medication and treatment. "Why would Victor disguise his symptoms? Didn't he want to get better?"

"That boy didn't think he was sick. Victor considered himself to be at the top of his game. He embraced his illness, thrived on it."

"Until he exploded."

Six years ago, Victor nearly beat an Iraqi prisoner to death. He'd faced a military trial and was on his way to a dishonorable discharge when he disappeared during a bombing and was listed as MIA.

Bart had done everything in his power to investigate his son's disappearance. But he failed. Every trail led to a dead end. The only logical conclusion was that Victor had been taken prisoner or was dead.

Though Bart seldom talked about his own tragedies, Nolan knew that Victor's supposed death affected him greatly. Because he'd lost his son, Bart dedicated himself to helping other military men returning from war.

"Thanks, Doctor. This is helping me understand."

"Victor wanted to prove something to his daddy. At the same time, he rejected Bart and everything he stood for."

In a surreal way, Victor's rationale made sense. When

he escaped his dishonorable discharge, he turned against the country he was sworn to protect. "Like a grudge."

"Damn right. He rambled on and on about people who deserved to die for what they'd done to him."

"Did he mention names?" Nolan asked.

"If he'd issued direct threats, I would have warned the people he'd targeted. He talked about a fiery she-devil and a brainless bastard. No names."

The fiery she-devil might be the redheaded nanny, Roxanne. Nolan hoped Amelia would have luck locating her. "A brainless bastard could be just about anybody."

Dr. Leigh barked a loud guffaw. "I like you, Nolan. Y'all look me up when you get back to town."

"Yes, sir. I will."

As he ended his call, Nolan ventured a small hope that by the time he returned to Freedom, this would all be settled. Bart would be safe. The CIA would have Greenaway in custody. And, most importantly, Tess and Joey would be with him.

Before leaving the study, he checked through the window to make sure her car was still in the parking area. His next job was to talk to her and to explain that she and Joey needed to stay here at Pierpont House. Convincing her wouldn't be easy. He needed to get her alone.

Winding through the corridors of the sprawling three-story house, he again wished that Bart was here. Tess would listen to Bart; she trusted him. In comparison, Nolan was a relative stranger.

In the large playroom, the kids had staked out their territories. One of the girls was dressed in a pink tutu while her identical twin sister wore jeans and a tiara on top of a Texas Rangers baseball cap. They had a tea party going near the kitchen. At the other end of the room, Joey and Zachary had assembled a fortress from sofa cushions and pillows. When Joey saw Nolan, he waved and came charging toward him.

Nolan hunkered down to meet his son. He wanted to grab the boy and hold him tight, but that wasn't his place. Not yet, anyway.

"How are you doing, Joey?"

"Great. We're having mac and cheese for lunch."

"That's my favorite."

"Me, too."

Nolan grinned. "Are you having fun?"

"Me and Zachary built a fort. No girls allowed."

Nolan looked toward Zachary, who stood motionless as a statue, watching Joey. "You better get back to your fort."

"Okay." He took off.

Nolan could feel Tess standing behind him. He knew she'd have questions about the abrupt way he'd departed from the sitting room. His best explanation was the truth—as much of the truth as he could tell.

He stood and pivoted to face her. "You've decided to let Joey stay for lunch."

"I didn't have much choice. As soon as he heard that it was macaroni and cheese, his decision was made." She glanced toward the fort. "He seems to be playing well with Stacy's son. She asked if Joey could spend the rest of the day here."

"Great idea." Convincing her might not be as difficult as he'd expected.

"But I can't. I have a million details to handle."

"All the more reason to leave Joey here," he said.

She gazed up at him. Her eyebrows arched. He knew that expression, knew that she was about to ask him a question. "When you dashed out of the room, you said you needed to talk to me. What's up?"

"It'll take a while to explain," he said. "I'll drive you to your appointments. We can talk in the car."

She considered for a moment. "I need to make a quick trip to the printer. That's not too far from here. We can do that while Joey has his mac and cheese. Then, back here."

"Let's go. Rock and roll."

Her lips tensed. "My husband used to say that. Must be a marine thing."

"Must be."

Chapter Ten

Irritated, Tess glared as the security guard brought Nolan's black Mercedes to the front door instead of her SUV. Damn it, she needed her car to pick up the materials from the printer. Taking the Mercedes was one more annoyance in a sting of frustrations that was beginning to tighten around her neck like a noose.

The last few days before any event were always hectic and fraught with problems. She expected trouble. Her role was to smile and smooth the waters, even when she felt like she was choking. Silently, she counted to five and turned her gaze toward the sky. The midday sun peeked through the clouds, and the temperature had warmed enough to melt last night's light snow. She exhaled slowly. *I'm fine. Everything is fine.*

As Nolan opened the passenger door for her, she spoke in the calmest tone she could manage. "I hope you have room in your trunk. There will be several heavy boxes."

"Of what?"

"Programs for the evening, place cards, menus, lists of honored guests."

"Can't you use a service for this pickup?"

"I want to double-check everything myself."

She watched Nolan as he came around the hood of the car. There was a slight hitch in his stride, probably the result of the surgeries he'd had on his left leg, but he moved with self-assurance. He radiated competence as though he could handle anything life threw at him.

The first time she'd seen him be less than supercool was earlier today when he'd dashed from the room where she and Lila had been meeting. He'd been shaken. His husky voice had been a taut whisper when he'd tossed out that cryptic comment. *We need to talk.* His tension was a bad sign, for sure. Nolan was a manly marine who'd been through hell. What could possibly be horrible enough to upset him?

It must be about Bart. Of course, she'd listen and she'd do whatever she could. Bart was the number one priority. Never mind that she was responsible for a high-toned dinner for three hundred at the Smithsonian. Correction: Three hundred and twenty-six. Lila had added guests.

As soon as Nolan was behind the steering wheel, she said, "Whatever is on your mind, I want to hear it right away. There simply isn't time for beating around the bush."

He hesitated. "It's better if I fill you in on the background."

Impatiently, she shook her head. "Just tell me. Right now. Straight up."

"It's about the name I saw on the Zamirs' guest list."

"Greenaway?"

"Has he been to other parties? Have you ever met him?"

"I don't recall the name. And we wouldn't have met. For the Zamir dinners in their home, I get things set up and then stay in the kitchen. They use the catering service I founded, and I like to lend a hand with the cooking." Enough said. "Who is this Greenaway person?"

"It's complicated." He turned the key in the ignition. "There are repercussions that will affect you."

"Okay." In her mind, she heard a clock ticking. "Cut to the chase."

"He's an international criminal."

"What?"

"You heard me." He pulled the car around the circular drive leading to the gates. "He's wanted by the CIA, NSA, Interpol and too many others to list."

"And he's coming to a dinner party that I'm planning? He's going to be eating my rosemary lamb chops?" Unbelievable! She chuckled. "I'd better hide my baklava recipe."

"This isn't a joke, Tess."

"How could this possibly affect me? I'm a party planner. Not somebody who gets involved in international intrigue."

He pulled to the side of the drive and parked. Turning to her, he removed his dark glasses. His expression was utterly serious. His gray eyes compelled her attention. "Greenaway is a threat to you. Both you and Joey are in danger."

The smile fell from her lips. She knew that Lila and her family had been targeted, but that was different. They were high-profile people. They had enemies. "Why me?"

"If you had allowed me to explain," he said, "you might understand."

"If I'd known what was coming, I wouldn't have been in such a hurry. You should have prepared me, Nolan. You jumped from we-need-to-talk to a death threat in two easy steps."

"You're not going to like what I have to say next." He slapped his sunglasses back on. "I want you and Joey to move to Pierpont House until the CIA has Greenaway in custody."

"Do you expect me to drop everything and move?"

"Yes."

"I can't. It's almost Christmas. I have a tree. I have Joey's presents." She paused to catch her breath. "And I have a business to run."

"I'll accompany you to your appointments."

"Like a bodyguard?"

"Exactly."

"What if I don't want a bodyguard? What if you're wrong about Greenaway?" Her irritation built into a solid rage. "You can't just swoop into my life and disrupt everything."

"Listen to me, Tess. You and your son are in danger. Precautions are necessary."

"This isn't your decision." She turned away from him and stared through the windshield. "I decide. And I need more information. Talk while you drive."

He slipped the car into gear and they rounded the curve to the front gate. The security guard gave them a wave as the gates opened electronically.

"It all started several years ago in Afghanistan," Nolan said. "Greenaway was making a deal with a couple of warlords to exchange illegal weapons for opium."

The inside of her head buzzed. The opium trade? Illegal weaponry? This story had no relevance in her life. None at all. *Nada.* Zero. Zip.

Nolan guided the Mercedes onto the street outside Pierpont House, a wide two-lane road with mini-mansions on spacious lots. There was no traffic and nobody walking. Expansive silence blanketed the neighborhood.

He continued, "When Bart was in the CIA, he had contact with Greenaway and others of his ilk. Disrupting their chain of distribution was one of his jobs."

She saw a shiny black SUV with a fancy silver grill and dark-tinted windows coming toward them. An obviously expensive vehicle, it belonged in this area as much as a purebred dog or a prize-winning rosebush.

Nolan reacted abruptly. He reached over and unsnapped her seat belt. "Get down."

"Why? What are—"

"Just do it, Tess. Get down behind the dashboard."

Responding to the urgency in his voice, she slid from her seat and curled up on the floor beside her briefcase. A sudden acceleration jostled her. They were moving fast. Nolan hit the brake. The tires squealed. The Mercedes spun in a one-eighty.

She felt an impact, but she didn't think they'd hit anything. They couldn't have. They were speeding too fast.

When she looked up, she saw Nolan's gun in his hand. His arm went out the open window. He fired several times. Someone else was shooting. She heard the cracking of glass. *This is real danger. I could be hurt.* Her gut tightened into a knot. She tasted bile in the back of her throat. If she was killed, what would happen to Joey?

The car jolted and swerved. She heard a loud scraping noise. Both front air bags exploded with a burst of white powder. The Mercedes came to a stop.

"Stay in the car," Nolan ordered.

He fought his air bag, flung open his door and jumped out. Bracing his gun in both hands, he fired.

She batted her air bag down, raised her head and peered over the dashboard. They were back inside the grounds. Both Nolan and the security guard were firing through the wrought iron gate. The windshield was marked with bullet holes and a spider's web of cracks. She glided her hand up the black leather passenger seat. Right where her head would have been was a hole.

This couldn't be happening, but it was. Here was proof. Nolan warned her. He told her the truth.

Panic coursed through her veins. *Joey, I have to get to Joey.* Her hand trembled violently, but she managed to grab the door handle and shove it open. Struggling to untangle her legs, she banged her knee but felt no pain. One thought hammered inside her head. *Joey. She had to rescue him.*

She staggered onto the circular driveway. The front door to the house opened and other men poured out. All were armed. This was a damn war zone.

Her head was spinning, she was cold and her legs were weak. With an odd detachment, she realized that she must be in shock. She wasn't physically injured but had been slammed with terror. Her strength was gone. She tripped, fell, scraped her knees on the driveway. A cry escaped her lips. She had to keep going, had to reach the house and make sure Joey was all right.

Strong hands grasped her shoulders. Nolan turned her toward him and pulled her close. He murmured, "It's all right, Tess. You're safe."

"Joey." She shoved against his chest. "I need to get to my son."

"Hush now. It's okay."

"Not okay. No, this is all wrong." A surge of energy went through her and she struggled. "Let go of me."

He held her at arm's length. His hands clamped around her upper arms. "Look at me, Tess. Listen to me."

She shook her head. Her brain rattled inside her skull. She felt tears spurting from her eyes.

"Come on, Tess. You don't want Joey to see you like this. You'll scare the hell out of him."

"Oh God, you're right." She was Joey's rock. Her son had no one else but her. She couldn't let him see her weakness. "What am I going to do?"

"You're going to let me take care of you and Joey. I'll

keep you safe. It's what I do." He released her arm and gently caressed her cheek. "Right now, we're going to the house. You'll go to the bathroom, wash your face and pull yourself together. Then, we'll talk to your son."

"And I'll tell Joey that we're staying here for a few days."

"That's the right decision."

She wiped away the remnants of tears. *I have to pull myself together.* Tess was an independent woman—a single mom who ran her own business. And yet, she found it strangely comforting when Nolan gave her directions. No thinking was required on her part. *Just do it.* She didn't have the strength to argue with him. All the fight had gone out of her.

When Tess emerged from the downstairs bathroom, she had regained a good part of her self-control. At least, she was capable of walking without falling over her own feet, and her tears had dried up.

She was glad to see Nolan waiting for her in the hallway with his arms folded across his chest and his back leaning against the wall. He'd taken off his sunglasses and hadn't put on the horn-rimmed spectacles. His unshielded gaze studied her as intently as a chef watching a soufflé, hoping it wouldn't collapse.

"You look fine," he told her.

Not exactly a rousing burst of encouragement. She'd washed her face, reapplied lipstick and brushed her hair. Luckily, she'd brought a change of clothes in her SUV in case it snowed. Nolan had fetched the more practical outfit—gray slacks that matched her suit jacket and sensible boots.

Concern for Joey remained uppermost in her mind, but

there were other worries. "This threat," she said, "does it extend to my business? Is Trudy safe?"

"She's not personally in danger," he said. "But it might be wise for her to stay away from your office."

"Are you sure this Greenaway person won't go after her?"

"As sure as I can be." He ushered her across the hall to a small study with a wall of books. Her briefcase rested on the desktop. "Why don't you give her a call?"

She stood behind the desk. "I learned my lesson, Nolan. I'm not going to rush you. Please give me a full explanation of why Trudy is safe."

"It's about Joe."

The breath went out of her lungs, and she sank into the swivel chair behind the desk. "My Joe?"

"Before he died, he had contact with Greenaway. Joe passed information to the CIA which ultimately led to Bart."

Bart had told her bits of the story. She knew he had worked with Joe and that was why he took such an interest in her and Joey. "Did Greenaway kill my husband?"

"His death wasn't targeted. Joe Donovan died in the explosion of a roadside bomb. But Greenaway never forgot. He's been keeping an eye on you and Joey through people like the Zamirs. That's why I'm sure Trudy is safe. Greenaway doesn't care about her."

She shuddered. For five years, she'd been under surveillance, and she'd never had a clue. "Why is he coming after me now?"

"Something big is going down, and Bart's involved. You're connected to Bart and to Lila and to CSaI. Killing you sends a message to the rest of us. Nobody's safe."

"I'm a pawn," she said. "Expendable."

"Never say that." His gray eyes warmed as he smiled.

"On my chessboard, you're the queen. You and Joey are first and foremost."

Another breakdown loomed in the back of her mind, but she pushed aside the fear and panic. She had too many responsibilities to indulge in emotion. "Before I talk to Trudy, I need to know if there's a way I can safely move around town."

"Since we prepared for threats to Lila, I have access to a bulletproof vehicle. Matt Soarez will ride shotgun. Literally."

"Much as I understand the need for protection, can you guys be subtle? I don't want to freak out the caterers."

"I can do subtle."

She rather doubted that Nolan would ever be able to fade into the woodwork. He was too overwhelmingly masculine to go unnoticed, as were the rest of the CSaI guys that she'd met.

As she flipped open her laptop and prepared to call Trudy, Nolan handed her a cell phone. "Use this. The signal is scrambled so no one can listen in."

"An espionage phone. Why am I not surprised?"

She reached Trudy at home and made an excuse for why she shouldn't go to the office until Tess could come with her. Then she divvied up the tasks for the day. The only jobs she had to handle personally were the printer and the caterer who was located in D.C. and closed at five o'clock.

And there was one more necessary stop. "We have to go to my house. Joey and I need clothes. And I'm sure he'll want some of his toys."

"We'll go there right after we talk to Joey."

Though it had been less than an hour since the assault on the Mercedes, her nerves had settled enough for her to slip into her mom role. When she entered the playroom with Nolan and saw her son, she felt the familiar rush of love and concern.

Her hug was tighter than usual but Joey didn't seem to notice the difference. He looked up at her and said, "Do we have to go?"

"Would you like to stay?"

"Yeah," he said with an energetic nod that caused his brown hair to flop over his forehead. "We're going to watch a movie this afternoon. A movie with horses. Lacey and Lyric have three dogs, and one of them herds cows. Can we go to Texas?"

"Maybe."

"I gotta meet these dogs."

Before he could jump into the I-want-a-dog discussion, she said, "I'm glad you're having a good time because we're going to stay here for a couple of days. It'll be a sleepover."

"You, too?"

"Me, too."

He frowned. "I don't know about that, Mommy."

"What's bothering you, kiddo?"

"It's almost Christmas. If I'm here, how is Santa Claus going to find me?"

Chapter Eleven

When Nolan heard Joey's question, he felt like laughing and crying at the same time. His four-year-old son believed in Santa, just like any other typical, normal kid. But Joey was *his* son. Therefore, his innocence touched a chord deep inside him. In this moment, Nolan knew what it meant to be a father.

He hunkered down to Joey's level. "Here's the deal with Santa Claus. He'll find you. He's got GPS. He knows where all the good boys and girls are."

"I'm very good," Joey said. "Aren't I, Mommy?"

"You certainly are."

Nolan nodded. "Your mom needs to do some running around this afternoon. You'll be okay while she's gone, right?"

"Yeah." Joey petted his mom's arm as though she was a kitty cat. "Mommy's good, too. She takes care of me. And I take care of her."

Tess kissed his forehead. "I'm going to run home and get some of our things. Is there anything you want?"

"Oh, yeah. My building blocks." He turned and yelled across the room to Zachary. "We're gonna build stuff."

"Anything else?" she asked.

He whispered, "Andy Panda. Don't tell the girls."

"Why not?"

"Because they'll treat him like a baby. Andy Panda is a boy. He doesn't wear dresses."

As the mother-son conversation continued, Nolan watched with awe. Tess was great with Joey, and vice versa. They took care of each other. *Because I wasn't around to help.* His son didn't know what it was like to have a father, and that was just plain wrong. Both he and Tess deserved to have a man around the house, and Nolan desperately wanted that job.

For now, he had to concentrate on the basics: keeping them both safe. He left Tess with her son for a few minutes while he found Matt Soarez and briefed him on their assignment for the afternoon.

"We're going to a caterer?" Soarez licked his lips. "What kind of food?"

"Hell if I know." Nolan couldn't care less. "Banquet food for Lila's big event."

"I suppose it's too much to hope for Tex-Mex."

In addition to being a decent cook, Soarez was handsome and charming—exactly the kind of bodyguard that Tess would want to have around while she did her errands. His only flaw was a pronounced limp from a gunshot wound to the leg that made him unfit for combat. Soarez liked to joke that he and Nolan were a matching set of gimps.

Together, they went around to the parking area and got the keys for the white bulletproof Hummer. The massive vehicle looked like a luxury SUV on steroids. Unless Greenaway's men came after them with RPGs, they ought to be safe.

"Can I drive?" Soarez asked.

"Knock yourself out."

While Nolan got in the passenger side, Soarez climbed

behind the wheel. He started the engine with a roar and paused to listen. "There's a lot of horses under that hood."

"I suppose." Nolan preferred cars that purred and wrapped around him.

"Me and the guys have been talking. And we're all wondering. What's the deal with you and Tess?"

"What do you mean?"

"You know what I'm saying. I've never seen you look at a woman the way you do with Tess. I even saw you take off the dark glasses."

"She's nice to look at." Nolan shrugged.

"If there's sparks, I'm all for it. It's about time you find a woman."

There was no way for him to explain that he'd found Tess long ago. Right now, they were getting reacquainted, and the process was trickier than anything he could have imagined. "Just drive."

Soarez pulled the Hummer around to the front entryway where Tess was waiting for them. Nolan hopped down from the passenger seat and came around to open the door to the rear.

"A giant white Hummer," she said drily. "Is this your idea of subtle?"

"It doesn't hurt for your caterer to know you're a badass."

She arched an eyebrow. "Clearly, you haven't met Pierre LeBrune. It would take more than a Hummer to intimidate him."

"Pierre who?"

"Exactly," she said.

As he joined her in the backseat, he introduced her to Matt Soarez. She reached between the seats to shake his hand. "Stacy tells me that your new wife owns the best eatery in Freedom, Texas."

"That's the truth." He flashed a brilliant white smile. "Talk of the Town Café has been in Faith's family for fifty years. She makes the world's greatest apple pie."

"I used to run a catering service," Tess said, "and I love to cook. I'm glad you're coming with us this afternoon. You might appreciate Pierre's work."

"What's his specialty?"

"He does incredible things with game birds. The appetizer for the Smithsonian event is a play on partridge in a pear tree."

Nolan was glad to see her return to her regular self—a little bit of smart aleck and a lot of warmth. After the shooting, she'd been a wreck. He suspected that she was still scared, but she did a damn fine job of covering up her emotions.

He remembered a long time ago—the night before he was shipping out for his second tour of duty in Afghanistan. She'd made a special candlelit dinner for him. When she'd raised her glass in a toast, she told him that she was scared about what might happen and angry that he was leaving her, but she didn't want to waste one precious minute of their time together.

The families who stayed behind were sometimes braver than the soldiers who left to do battle, braver and stronger.

He tuned back in to her conversation with Soarez.

"I've got to tell you," Tess said, "I'm a little worried about Pierre."

"How come?"

"He wasn't happy about using the beef supplier the governor wanted. I'm afraid he's going to blow his top when I tell him he has to add twenty-six guests. Maybe you can distract him by talking about partridges."

Nolan's cell phone rang. The caller ID showed it was

the CSaI uffice. When Amelia answered, she sang instead of talking. "Roxanne. Roxanne. Roxanne."

"You already have information," he said.

"That's right. I'm astounding, thank you very much."

"Hold on." Nolan looked toward Tess. "Tess, why don't you sit up front so you can give directions. I need to take this call."

"No problem." She wedged through, sat on the passenger side and fastened her seat belt.

In the back of the Hummer, Nolan stayed on alert, watching for threats. It was unlikely that Greenaway's men would repeat their earlier effort, but he wanted to know if they were being tailed.

He held the cell phone to his ear. "Okay, Amelia. What can you tell me about Roxanne?"

"Bart hired her through a nanny service based near Langley. One of his CIA buddies must have referred him."

Langley was only a couple of miles outside Washington, D.C., in Virginia. "She was from around here."

"A local gal," Amelia said. "Her last name used to be Wachovski, which is unusual enough that she was easy to track. You have no idea how difficult it is to get information on a Smith or a Jones. The average names kind of blend together, but a red-headed Roxanne Wachovski is a standout."

Though he was anxious for her to get to the point, namely Roxanne's current address and phone number, Nolan said nothing. Amelia was famous for her quirky, convoluted explanations. Interrupting would only send her off on another tangent.

"After she left Bart, Roxanne had another couple of nanny jobs. When she got married and changed her name, she opened a child care business. That didn't last and neither did the marriage. She went back to her maiden name."

"And then?" he prompted.

"She still takes the occasional nanny assignment, but she's getting a little old to be chasing kids around. She's in her early sixties, and she's a Scorpio."

"Is her astrology sign relevant?"

"Always," Amelia said. "For example, you're an Aries, which means stubborn, determined and…"

She was off and running. Babbling on about how the designs of the stars influenced our lives. Nolan looked toward the front seat where Soarez and Tess discussed the relative merits of mesquite grilling.

There was too much noise. How the hell had life gotten so complicated? He wanted to explode the confusion and make it simple. He needed to find Bart, end Greenaway and make Tess and Joey part of his life. Not necessarily in that order.

"I'll bet," Amelia said, "you're ready to hear the big, fat, exciting conclusion to the tale of Roxanne."

"I am."

"She still lives in a suburb near Langley."

"Amelia, you're a genius."

"I know."

She gave him the address and phone number, and then asked, "How's the hotel?"

"It's okay."

She scoffed. "It should be five stars better than okay. It's the suite Bart uses when he's in Washington."

That explained the opulence of the two-bedroom suite. Bart was a wealthy man who could afford to indulge. For Nolan, the high-class ambience was a waste. He only used the room for sleeping.

He ended the call just as Soarez parked outside the printer. Before exiting the Hummer, they checked their weapons. He and Soarez had worked together before as bodyguards. They might be gimps, but they had their movements perfected. With Tess sandwiched between them, they rushed across the sidewalk into the plain store-front.

The skinny young man at the front counter gave Tess a friendly greeting, but it was clear that he didn't know what to make of her two companions in dark glasses with shoulder holsters. His voice squeaked, "Is everything okay?"

"It's all fine," Tess assured him. "Can we go into the back room to proofread?"

Soarez stayed at the front to keep an eye on the door while Nolan accompanied Tess into a small room with a big window looking out at the store. He sat beside her. "I can help. I've been over the guest list with Lila, so I know most of the names."

"You read," she said. "I'll check."

The proofreading process was the same as when they sent out their wedding invitations. Though they'd kept the ceremony simple and within a budget, they had invited two hundred friends and family. As they fell into the pattern, he wondered how she thought about their life together. He knew she mourned the death of Joe Donovan. But did she ever look back on the good times? What stood out in her mind?

Most often, he recalled the little things. Seeing her patent leather high heels on the floor beside the bed. Hearing her sing off-key in the shower. Watching her sleep. He had never taken her for granted. From the start, he'd known that he was blessed.

It was becoming clear that he had to tell her who he was. The longer he kept the secret, the harder it would be to finally pull back the curtain and reveal the truth. He knew she'd be angry. He hoped she'd forgive him.

Looking down at the list of names, he lost his place for

a moment. "The next one is Leonard O'Malley with an 'e'."

She flipped through the place cards until she found the name, then she checked her wristwatch and frowned. "This is taking too long. It's already after two o'clock."

"If we leave by three, there's still enough time to get into the city and see your caterers."

"I'm not sure it's necessary." She leaned back in the plastic chair and stared up at the ceiling. "These people have catered other events at the Smithsonian. They come highly recommended. By checking their preparations, I might be acting like an annoying micromanager."

"You could never be annoying."

She slowly lowered her gaze and looked at him. Her smile was sly and adorable. "Nolan, you have no idea."

But he did, of course. He'd been the guy who drove her all over town to look for a specific fresh herb. He'd been the taster who tried six varieties of vanilla cupcake before picking the one that had the best flavor. "You're a perfectionist. Nothing wrong with that."

"I was almost killed today." A hint of fear flashed in her eyes. "That's a wake-up call that can't be ignored. I'm too intense about my career."

"Because you're good at it."

"I am. I definitely am. Frankly, every detail of Lila's event is already planned. Even if I don't race all over town checking and double-checking, there's a ninety percent chance that everything will be fine." She tapped on the tabletop with her right forefinger as though pointing out the obvious. "I need to focus on what is really, truly important."

"Joey," he said.

"And finding Bart." She confronted him again. "That phone call you had to take was about him, wasn't it?"

He gave a quick nod. "I have an address and phone number for Victor's former nanny."

"When you meet with her, I want to come along."

"Every time you leave Pierpont House, you're in danger."

"Are you absolutely sure about that? I've been thinking, and it occurred to me that the bad guys didn't really know it was me in the car with you. They might have been coming after Lila or somebody else."

Greenaway's men wouldn't make such a rookie mistake. "Don't kid yourself. They knew your identity."

"How? They were halfway down the block."

"Current developments in long-range vision technology allow clear sight for over two hundred yards."

"Long-range vision?"

"Binoculars," he said. "Think of binoculars that are a million times more powerful than anything you've ever looked through."

"Oh."

"I understand that you want to be involved, but you're a civilian. The best thing for you to do is stay safe."

"We'll see." She stood and gathered up the documents they'd been proofreading. "I can finish this later. Right now, I want to go to my house and pick up a few things. Tomorrow is soon enough to meet with the caterer."

Though he was a supposedly determined Aries, Nolan was no match for Tess when she'd made a decision. All he could do was follow in her wake and make sure she wasn't injured while she plunged forward.

For the ride to her house, she stayed in the backseat of the Hummer with him while Soarez drove using the GPS for directions to her house. Tess took the opportunity to point out that she'd been helpful when he talked to Lila. Wouldn't she be equally helpful in dealing with Roxanne?

Send For
2 FREE BOOKS
Today!

I accept your offer!

Please send me two
free Harlequin Intrigue®
novels and two mystery
gifts (gifts worth about $10).
I understand that these books
are completely free—even
the shipping and handling will
be paid—and I am under no
obligation to purchase anything, ever,
as explained on the back of this card.

❏ I prefer the regular-print edition
182/382 HDL FH74

❏ I prefer the larger-print edition
199/399 HDL FH74

Please Print

FIRST NAME

LAST NAME

ADDRESS

APT.#   CITY

STATE/PROV.   ZIP/POSTAL CODE

Visit us online at
www.ReaderService.com

The nanny might be more willing to open up with another woman.

"You're kind of intimidating," she said.

"It works for me," he said. "People know I'm not kidding around. They'll do what I want."

She raised her hand to cover a grin.

"What?" he asked. "Did I say something funny?"

"You're not as scary as you think you are. Joey had your number from the minute you walked in the door. Within a minute of meeting you, he'd wangled an invitation to take him horseback riding in Texas."

From the front seat, Soarez called out, "You got it right, Tess. Nolan is a pussycat."

"Just keep your eyes on the road," Nolan growled.

"We're here."

Soarez pulled into the driveway and parked. Since her house was a likely target for Greenaway's men, they took extra precautions in their approach. Leaving Tess inside the Hummer, Nolan and Soarez went to the back door and entered with their guns drawn and ready.

Nolan moved through the kitchen into the living room.

Greenaway had already been here.

The house was ransacked.

Tess was going to be furious.

Chapter Twelve

Tess stood in the middle of her living room, shocked and angry. Slowly, she turned in a circle. Everywhere she looked was another example of heedless destruction. She really didn't mind that the sofa cushions had been slashed. Replacing that piece of furniture had been on her agenda. But she hated to see her cherished mementos scattered and broken.

These intruders, these vandals, these monsters had attacked her Christmas tree. The poor thing lay on its side with the multicolored lights blinking sadly through the tinsel. The ornaments were strewn about. The angel that topped the tree had lost her halo and her wings.

She had pleasant memories attached to some of the decorations. But none had great monetary value. Nor were they irreplaceable. The damage was senseless, which made it even more infuriating.

Turning her back on the tree, she went toward the roll-top desk. The photograph of her and Joe in the Bahamas had been torn from the wall. She bent her knees and picked it up. The glass was shattered as though the intruders had stomped on it with heavy boots.

The glass could be replaced. Most of the damage could be repaired, but she would never forget how she felt in this moment. Vicious strangers had violated her home. Any doubts she had about being the intended victim were gone.

Nolan stood beside her. "I have to ask you not to touch anything. There might be fingerprints or trace evidence."

"Did you call the police?"

"The CIA," he said. "Omar Harris and a forensic team are on their way. They have access to the best labs in the country. They'll find who did this."

"Thank God I didn't bring Joey home."

"I'll get everything put back together before he sees it," Nolan said. "I promise you that."

She gently placed the broken picture frame on the roll-top desk. "What were they looking for?"

"I don't know."

When she took a step, glass crunched under her boot heel. She didn't want to mess up the possible evidence, but this was her house. The idea of having Omar and a team of CIA specialists pawing through her things was only slightly less disturbing than the original assault.

Looking down the hallway, she clenched her jaw. "How bad are the bedrooms?"

"Torn up," Nolan said. "Not much is broken."

"I need to get a few things for me and Joey. If that's a problem for the CIA, I don't give a damn."

He didn't object. "Take whatever you need. I'll help."

In the bedroom, her clothing had been rifled through and dumped on the floor. The mattress on the king-size bed she'd once shared with her husband had been tossed off the box springs. She reached under the bed and grasped the edge of a black plastic garbage bag which she pulled out.

Immediately, she looked inside. "I'm glad they didn't find this."

"What is it?"

"Joey's Christmas presents. And there's a two-wheel bike with training wheels in the garage." She lifted her chin. "I'm taking these things with me."

"No argument."

Soarez came into the room with another big plastic bag. "I'm sorry, Tess, but the CIA won't want you to remove anything from the crime scene."

"It's my house." She didn't mean to snap at him, but couldn't help herself. "Before it was a crime scene, I lived her with my son. With my husband. Joe and I bought this house. We furnished it." .

Her anger was building toward a full-scale explosion with lava shooting from the top of her head. This wasn't fair. She'd done nothing wrong. She didn't deserve this.

Nolan's voice was gentle. "You're right to be mad."

"Oh, good, because I don't think I can stop myself."

"But you need to be practical. Let's get the stuff you need and get out before the forensic people arrive." He snapped a black plastic bag open. "Start with your clothes."

She'd always been a careful packer, the kind of person who rolled her shirts and used tissue paper to prevent wrinkles. But this was an emergency. She grabbed what she might need for the next few days and threw it into the bag. "All of these things have to be washed before I can wear them."

"There's a laundry service at Pierpont House," Nolan said.

From the floor in the closet, she grabbed the brand-new emerald silk cocktail dress she'd purchased for the dinner at the Smithsonian. Since it was still in the plastic bag from the store, she wouldn't have to clean it. She tossed in shoes, including comfortable sneakers, and jackets and shirts. "That's enough."

Nolan handed the bag of Joey's presents to Soarez. "Put this in the Hummer. There's also a brand-new two-wheeler in the garage."

Joey's room was less chaotic than the rest of the house. A few things had been tossed around, and the drawers in his dresser hung open. She made sure that she took the two large containers for his building blocks. And she scooped up a bunch of his clothes. Her son wouldn't care if he wore the same shirt for three or four days, but she cared. She also took his dress-up suit in case had to come along with her for the Smithsonian event.

"Is that everything?" Nolan asked. "We need to hurry."

"Andy Panda." She looked on the bed where the raggedy stuff animal usually sat. "I don't see it."

"What does it look like?"

"Black and white, obviously. It's about the size of a fat squirrel and kind of mangled. Andy Panda is Joey's favorite thing to sleep with. Bart gave it to him."

A horrible thought occurred to her. "What if Bart hid something in the stuffed animal? Some kind of microchip or a secret flash drive or something."

"Or not," Nolan said.

"It makes sense." She gestured to Joey's room. "They didn't make as much of a mess in here. If they were looking for Andy Panda, they'd stop searching when they found it."

"You've been watching too many spy movies." He reached behind the end of the bed and fished around, then he felt against the wall until he pulled the black-and-white toy. "Is this the panda in question?"

"Thank you, Mr. Law." She snatched it from his hand and stalked toward the door. "Let's rock and roll."

SAFELY BACK AT Pierpont House, Tess knew she'd made the right decision about rescheduling the meeting with the caterer. She wasn't fit to do business; her emotions were all over the place. Angry and scared. Perplexed and defiant. You name it, she felt it. Most of all, she was fiercely maternal, watching over Joey as he played with the other kids. How was she going to tell him that someone had broken into their house? Did he need to know? Could she just pretend that everything was all right?

Though she wanted to believe the situation couldn't get worse, she remembered the old adage: Bad things come in threes. What else? What the hell else could go wrong?

She managed to hold it together long enough for a phone call to Trudy, who had checked in with the florist, the ice sculptor and the bakery that was creating a four-foot-tall cake replicating the Alamo with figures of Davy Crockett and Jim Bowie. Preparations for the Smithsonian event seemed to be on track, but Tess couldn't help worrying. Another disaster was lurking; she could feel it coming closer.

After checking out the third-floor bedroom where she and Joey would be staying, she got their clothes started in the laundry room. Then she joined Stacy and Lindsay in the kitchen where they were supervising the kids while they made Christmas cookies.

Though Tess was an experienced caterer, she didn't offer any advice about the recipe or the crazy way the kids decorated the sugar cookies. This exercise wasn't about being gourmet. It was fun for the kids.

Stacy and Lindsay were lighthearted. Both were caught in the throes of new love with their mates, and neither of them had expected to find such passion. Only a few months ago, they had both been single moms like Tess.

While the kids smeared green and red frosting, she stepped back to lean against the counter beside the other moms. This was a good opportunity for her to dig up some dirt on Nolan. "I know the basics about him," she said. "But what's his personal life like? Has he ever been married? What's his story?"

"Your guess is as good as mine." Lindsay shrugged. She was a rancher—the kind of woman who put absolutely no effort into grooming her long auburn hair but still looked gorgeous.

"He gives a whole new definition to strong and silent," Stacy said. "Nolan isn't big on sharing. I think there was some horrible tragedy in his past."

"Something more horrible than being blown up in Afghanistan?" Tess asked.

Stacy lowered her voice so the kids wouldn't hear. "I think there was a woman. Somebody he loved and lost."

"One thing is for sure," Lindsay said, "Nolan is the alpha dog. He's second-in-command after Bart, and the other guys look up to him, even though he's not much older than anybody else."

"CSaI is his life," Stacy confirmed. "He's like a son to Bart."

Tess suspected that Bart would prefer a son like Nolan Law, a man who was a hero and generated automatic respect from his coworkers. Victor must have been a disappointment.

"Nolan likes you," Lindsay said. "I've never seen him so smitten."

"I like him, too." She smiled. "And so does Joey."

"So important," Stacy said. "Harlan is much better with Zachary than his father ever was. By the way, Tess, your boy is wonderful with Zachary. I mean, look at them."

Zachary and Joey had pretty much given up on decorating the cookies and were painting each other with icing.

"They're something else, all right. Do you mind helping Joey wash up while I get my laundry?"

"I'm happy to watch Joey," Stacy said, "but you don't have to mess with the laundry. Let the service handle it."

"I don't mind doing it myself."

In fact, she was looking forward to spending a few moments alone. After she gathered up their clothes, she climbed the back stairway to their bedroom on the third floor. Sorting and folding the laundry made her feel like she was creating a nest, a place where she and Joey would be cozy and safe.

She hung the last of their clothes in the small closet, placed Andy Panda in the middle of his twin bed and smoothed the quilt. Even the tiny spare bedroom in this house was nicely decorated with two brass frame beds, a dresser and a small window.

Long ago when the house was first built, the third floor had probably been the servant's quarters. The layout reminded her of a dormitory with four small bedrooms on either side of a long hallway. On this floor, there were only two bathrooms—one at each end of the hall.

Joey bounded through the door and dove onto the bed. "Mommy? Are you okay?"

"I'm fine, kiddo."

"Why are we staying here?"

How much should she tell him? She remembered when he started asking questions about his father's death. That talk had been incredibly hard, and this was equally complicated. She wouldn't lie, that much was certain. But she couldn't dump the whole truth on him. Joey was a kid. There wasn't much he could do to help her, and she didn't want to burden him with more than he could handle.

She sat on the bed beside him and started in. "There are some bad things happening."

"Like Bart," he said. "You said that he went away and you can't find him."

"That's right. Bart didn't want to go away, but he had to." She wanted to add that Bart would come back, but she couldn't be sure. "We're trying to find him."

"You and Mr. Law," he said.

"And many other people, too. Zachary's dad and the twins' dad and everybody. We all love Bart."

He grabbed Andy Panda, rolled onto his back and held the stuffed toy close so he could look into the button eyes. "Don't worry, Andy Panda. We'll find Bart."

Joey always leaned toward the positive, and she was grateful for that. He was also as straightforward as an arrow. He scowled at her. "What's the bad stuff?"

"First off, I want you to know that none of this is your fault. And it's not my fault, either. We just got caught up in somebody else's problems." She was at a loss to explain why an international bad guy wanted revenge on them because of a long-ago incident involving Joe. And she didn't want to frighten Joey. "Mr. Law and I decided it was best for you and me to stay here until the bad guys are caught."

He thought for a minute. "Okay."

Relieved, she grinned. "I liked what you said earlier. That you take care of me and I take care of you."

"We take care of us." He bounced off the bed. "Mommy, is it okay if I don't sleep here tonight?"

"Have you made other plans?"

"Me and Zachary built a fort downstairs, and we wanted to camp in it. His mom said we could have marshmallows."

"That sounds fun. It's okay with me."

He replaced Andy Panda on the bed and zoomed into the hallway. Joey's resilience was the number one best thing that had happened all day. In second place was Lindsay's comment that Nolan liked her.

At her age, it was silly to be excited about a man showing interest. Thirty-six-year-old women didn't have crushes or doodle their boyfriend's name in a notebook. Would she even call Nolan a boyfriend? He definitely wasn't a boy.

Speaking of the devil, he knocked on the doorframe. "May I come in?"

"Please do."

In the small room, his shoulders seemed huge. He filled the space with his presence. When she looked up at him, the waning afternoon light through the window reflected off his horn-rimmed glasses.

"We've located Roxanne."

"What did she say about Victor?"

"Nothing yet." His rasping, smoky voice coiled around her. "Wade Coltrane talked to her on the phone while he was sitting in his car right outside her house. She told him she didn't want to meet at her home."

"Does that mean she knows something?"

"It might," he said. "Coltrane set up a meeting with her at eight o'clock in the bar at the Viceroy Hotel."

"Nice place." The Viceroy was small, exclusive and super deluxe. Tess knew where it was but had never been inside.

"I have a suite there," he said. "It's where Bart stays when he's in town. Since he isn't here, I get the fancy room."

Thinking about Nolan and hotel rooms—or Nolan in a luxury hotel suite—started her imagination running. There would be amenities and room service and Egyptian cotton sheets…and him. "And why are you telling me this?"

"Roxanne is obviously skittish. I thought it might be good for you to come along. Like you said, she might be more open with another woman."

She sensed a deeper meaning. "Is that the only reason?"

"I like being with you."

Though he was careful not to crowd her, he was still too close—easily within kissing range. Hadn't she just told him that she wanted to go slow?

"Yes," she said. "I'll come with you."

Chapter Thirteen

In person, Roxanne Wachovski was prettier than Nolan expected. The ID photo on her driver's license—which Amelia had provided for them—made her look hard in spite of her curly auburn mane. Amelia had pointed out that she'd shaved off a couple of years on her ID and said she was forty-nine.

"She's here," he said to Tess.

Sitting at a small round table in the Viceroy Hotel bar, they'd been waiting for Roxanne for twenty minutes. That might have been the perfect time for him to have a serious conversation with her, but they weren't really alone. Nolan was connected via a tiny two-way communication device to Wade Coltrane, who had been tailing Roxanne in case she changed her mind about talking and decided to bolt.

With Wade listening to every word he said, Nolan had kept the conversation simple—focusing on the Smithsonian event and Christmas and Joey. He'd told Tess that when they were done with Roxanne, he'd hide Joey's Christmas presents in his hotel suite where her son couldn't accidentally stumble over them. That gave him the excuse he needed to get her by herself.

And then, he'd say the words he should have said when he first walked into her office. Tonight, he would tell her the whole truth. After what she'd been through today, she deserved to know his identity.

He raised his hand and signaled to Roxanne, who sauntered across the room, swinging her hips. She was round and soft—heavier than the weight recorded on her ID, but in a good way. When she unbuttoned her winter coat, she showed cavernous cleavage.

"I'll have a pinot grigio," she said as she sat.

"Coming right up," he said. "My name is Nolan Law. This is Tess Donovan."

"Are you CIA? Military intelligence?" Through gobs of mascara, she squinted at him. "What kind of spy are you?"

"I work for a private security firm founded by Bart Bellows," Nolan said as he fastened a listening device to the underside of the table so he could overhear anything Roxanne said to Tess while he was out of earshot.

Tess introduced herself, "I'm a party planner. I'm here because Bart is a good friend of mine."

"A special friend?" Roxanne said with a leer. "Maybe, a lover?"

"Just a friend," Tess said definitely. "He helped me through a difficult time. I love him like an uncle."

"Yeah, I supposed Bart's getting too old to chase the ladies. Not that he ever made a pass at me. Believe me, I tried to get him interested. He was a catch. Richer than Trump and not bad to look at." She looked toward Nolan. "I thought you were getting my drink."

He went to the bar, listening through the bug as Roxanne continued to talk to Tess.

"What's this about?" the redhead demanded. "The guy on the phone mentioned Victor Bellows."

Tess hesitated. "We should wait until Nolan comes back."

"I want you to tell me. I trust you more than those tough guys."

"Okay," Tess said, "Bart has been kidnapped, and we think Victor is responsible."

She swore under her breath. "Doesn't surprise me. Victor Bellows is a bad seed. Know what I mean? He was born to make trouble."

From the bar, Nolan watched the two women. They made an interesting contrast. Roxanne was earthy and sensual. Tess was…an angel. Her pale skin actually seemed to glow, and her black hair shimmered in the dim lights of the hotel bar.

"I don't get it," Roxanne said. "Why did these guys contact me?"

"We're trying to get as much information on Victor as we can. You were his nanny when he was a preteen. You might remember something about him that could be helpful."

Nolan returned to the table with her wine and set the glass in front of her. "We've spoken to Lila Lockhart. She remembered that Victor used to play tricks on you."

"It wasn't the usual mischief," Roxanne said with a shudder. "He was a disturbed kid. He really wanted to hurt me. Or scare me. He put spiders in my bed. And a snake. I couldn't close my eyes for one minute."

"When was the last time you saw him?" Nolan asked.

"Two years ago." She lifted her glass and took a long sip. "I can tell you some really interesting things about that creep. First, I need something from you."

"Name it," he said.

"I need your assurance that Victor will never know that I talked to you. I don't want him showing up on my doorstep looking for revenge."

"Everything you say will be confidential."

She took another hit of wine. "And I want to know what's in it for me."

"You could be helping us save Bart's life," he said.

"Oh sure, it's the right thing to do. Taking another psychopath off the streets, blah, blah, blah." Her eyes narrowed. "I'm not getting any younger. I need to think of my retirement. This info is going to cost you."

"Five thousand," Nolan said. He had that much in his checking account. "I'll have it transferred to your bank in the morning."

"That's good for a start," she said.

"If Bart comes through this in one piece, he'll be in your debt."

"And Bart is a very wealthy man." Roxanne considered for a moment. "I'll talk, Nolan. But not to you. I'm going to have a chat with Tess. You can run along."

He saw Roxanne's confidence; she thought she was calling the shots. But he also sensed her fear. Two years ago, Victor had scared her, and Nolan wanted to know that story. He rose from the table. "I'll wait at the bar."

Though Roxanne lowered her voice, he heard her clearly through the bug.

"I hadn't stayed in touch with Victor, never thought I'd see him again, and that was fine with me. I spent two years being his nanny because Bart paid me twice what I'd make at any other job. But I quit when Victor turned fifteen. He was a big kid, and he was starting to get threatening."

"Did he ever hurt you?"

"I can show you the scars. Victor was a sicko."

"Actually, I think you're right," Tess said. "He has an illness. Did he ever get treatment or medication?"

"Bart didn't want anything that would cause a blemish on Victor's record. He thought the boy was acting out because of his mother's death. But he did take him to a doctor—an off-the-record doctor—who provided medication. And it helped. Victor calmed down."

Her statement fit with what Nolan had heard from Dr. Leigh. Apparently, Victor had a chemical imbalance that caused him to behave badly. But he was treatable.

"He didn't like the pills," Roxanne said. "He quit taking them. One day, he flew into an uncontrollable rage. The only thing I could do was lock him in the basement of the house. I called Bart and got the hell away from there."

Tess prompted, "And when you saw him two years ago?"

"He and another guy were standing on my doorstep. They were polite, said they were looking for a lost dog. I didn't recognize Victor right away. He was over six feet tall and all filled out. It wasn't until I invited them inside that I looked into his eyes, those crazy blue eyes. Then I knew him. But it was too late. He slapped me hard, knocked me on my ass. And he kicked me. It was awful. I thought I was a dead woman."

"I'm so sorry."

Nolan watched as Tess reached across the table and rested her hand on Roxanne's arm. Her empathy was real. And it served a purpose. He knew that Tess would be able to get more information from this woman than he could.

"The other guy with him," Tess said, "did he just stand by and watch?"

"He was worse than Victor. He yanked me off the floor and shoved me against the wall. He was going to rape me, but Victor told him not to. Victor said he was on a mission. He was going to pay back everybody who wronged him. And he thought that included me."

"Did Victor say the other guy's name?"

"Elliot." She shuddered. "A real creep. I think they went to high school together."

"What made you think that?"

"Elliot talked about their gang. The Recluses."

"Not a very scary name," Tess said. "A recluse likes to be left alone. Maybe they thought they were outcasts."

"That fits," Roxanne said. "I sure didn't want anything to do with either of them."

Nolan turned away from the table and spoke so Coltrane could hear him. "The name is Elliot. Does that match up with any of Victor's high school friends?"

"I'm checking the list," Coltrane said. "There were four guys expelled. None named Elliot."

"Contact Amelia and have her expand the search to include his whole class and his teachers. Tell her to look for the Recluse gang."

"It's a good lead. If Elliot is still in the area, Victor could be staying with him."

Nolan hoped so. It would be better for Bart if Victor was holed up with a high school buddy. If Victor had turned his father over to Greenaway, Bart didn't stand a chance.

Through the bug, he heard Tess talking. "You said that Victor thought attacking you was part of a mission. What else did he say about his revenge?"

"He and Elliot had already done something terrible to their former principal's new car. They talked about an explosion and laughed. Victor got right in my face and told me that he'd learned about more than setting bombs when he was in Afghanistan. He'd learned how to inflict pain."

"You must have been terrified."

"Hell, yes. And he said the worst suffering wasn't physical. He talked about how his father hurt him without touching him. Victor wanted to get even."

Tess asked, "How did you get away from him?"

"He tied my wrists and ankles. Then he shoved me into

the basement of my house and nailed the door shut. He said this was my just punishment. If I reported it to the police, he'd be back."

"Did you?" Tess asked. "Did you call the police?"

"No way. It took me a couple of hours to get out, and I considered myself lucky to be alive. I never told anybody. Until now."

"I appreciate your help," Tess said.

"Just make sure that Bart knows what I did." Roxanne finished the dregs of her wine. "Maybe it's just as well that nothing worked out between me and Bart. I don't think I could handle being Victor's stepmother."

Nolan doubted that any sane woman would sign up for that job. If Bart hadn't been the toughest son-of-a-gun that he'd ever known, he might not have survived as Victor's father.

Nolan couldn't push the nagging fear to the back of his mind. Victor's revenge might have already overtaken Bart. There was no guarantee that he was still alive.

TESS ENTERED NOLAN'S suite carrying the black trash bag that held Joey's already wrapped Christmas presents. For a moment, she stood and stared. The central room was as large as the living room and dining room of her house. Every flat surface had an arrangement of flowers suitable for the Christmas season—winter roses in white and green, pine boughs and poinsettias. On a large oblong meeting table was a fruit basket that had been unwrapped but was mostly uneaten.

"Fabulous." She meandered past the sofa and green striped chairs, ran her fingers along the polished cherry tables and side tables. The twelfth floor windows had an incredible view of the Washington Monument.

By some decorating marvel, the posh antique ambience

of the room wasn't ruined by the massive flat-screen television hanging on the wall over a credenza. She opened a door on the left side to a full-size bedroom with a king-size, four-poster bed. One of her favorite luxuries was bedding. The duvet was fine linen, pale green. When she caressed one of the pillows, she recognized Egyptian cotton with a thread count in the thousands. Lying on these sheets would be like floating on a cloud.

She opened another door. "And it's a walk-in closet. There's only one lonely suit hanging in here."

"For the Smithsonian thing," he said.

"Really? I thought I might talk you into playing Santa."

"Not while I'm doing security. A shoulder holster doesn't fit with a red suit and fake beard."

Since Joey was playing campout with Zachary, she didn't feel like she had to rush back to the Pierpont House to take care of him. If any problem arose, Stacy would call her. Tess was free for the night.

"Can I get you a drink?" Nolan asked.

"Any red wine is okay for me."

She followed him into the central room. Here she was… in a fabulous hotel suite…with a man she was attracted to. If tonight followed a natural progression, she might end up in that bed, tangled in Egyptian cotton sheets with Nolan.

Did she dare? There wasn't any possibility of a relationship. After the Christmas Eve event, he'd be heading back to Texas. They probably wouldn't see each other again, which meant that tonight was a one-night stand. If she could get away tomorrow, it might be two nights. And that wasn't her style.

Tess was responsible and careful. And she hadn't made love for five years. She could count on one hand—on two fingers, actually—the number of men who had kissed her since her husband died.

Nolan placed the wineglass in her hand. "It's chilled. There's a mini-fridge under the wet bar."

"Of course there is." She lifted her glass in a toast. "Here's to you for being so clever and planting a bug at the table so I wouldn't have to repeat Roxanne's story."

"You're the clever one." He clinked the rim of his glass against hers. "You did a great job with her, asking all the right questions."

She took a sip. "Good wine."

"Good company."

"What happens next?" she asked. "How is this Elliot person significant?"

"If Victor is in town and isn't directly connected with Greenaway, he needs a place to stay. He might look up his old buddy, Elliot."

"Do you think Bart is with Victor?"

"I wish I knew."

Remembering what Roxanne had said about Victor's revenge mission and his father, Tess feared for Bart's safety. "We've got to hope for the best."

He sat close to her on the sofa and placed his wineglass on the coffee table. "You've been through a lot."

"Everybody has their own set of tragedies. That's life."

"I want to make it better." He slipped off his horn-rimmed glasses and set them on the table beside the half-full glass of wine. "I want you to be happy."

Her gaze sank into his gray eyes. She was mesmerized by the gentle warmth reflected in the prisms and facets of his irises. His eyes were so familiar. Had she dreamed of him last night? Had she known him before they met?

She took another sip of the red wine. Her glass joined his on the table. She wanted her hands free. Reaching toward him, she traced a long scar on the left side of his face. His skin was rough and mottled. "Did I ever thank you for saving my life?"

"It's not necessary."

He leaned toward her. She closed her eyes and waited for him to kiss her. Her heartbeat fluttered. The anticipation was killing her.

Their lips met.

She had been kissed like this before. Exactly like this. Every night for five years, she had dreamed of this moment. She knew the pressure of his mouth, his taste, his smell.

It was him.

"Joe?"

Chapter Fourteen

Tess kept her eyes closed. She had no idea how or why this miracle had occurred, but she didn't want it to end.

His voice was a whisper. "Tess, I need to—"

"Don't talk."

Blindly, she rubbed her hands on his chest as though reassuring herself that he was real and not a ghost. The material of his sweater bunched under her fingers and she pulled him closer. Her fingers slipped past the collar of his shirt and rested at the base of his throat. She felt his pulse and the heat from his body. *Is this really happening?*

For five long and desperate years, she'd been alone. She was a widow, a single mom. Those years were a famine. And now, she was hungry. She wanted to touch every part of him—on the inside and on the surface. He was back. Joe had come back to her.

Am I losing my mind? Logically, this could not be. She reached higher until she was holding his face in her hands. Eyes still closed, she kissed him again. *Oh my God, it was him.* She knew. Without the slightest doubt, she knew. He was the love of her life, her soul mate, the father of her son.

Too much, this was way too much. She couldn't take it. She leapt to her feet. "Stay here."

"What are you doing?"

"Just stay."

She ran into the adjoining bedroom and closed the door. *Settle down, Tess. Get a grip.* The inside of her head was whirling like an insane carousel with flashing lights and screeching music.

Leaning against the door, she tried to steady herself. Her breath came in shallow gasps; she couldn't get enough oxygen to her brain. Darkness pushed at the edge of her vision, threatening to overwhelm her. She was on the verge of fainting dead away.

He tapped on the door. "Are you all right?"

"What do you think?"

She'd just experienced the shock of a lifetime. The world had turned upside down. He was alive, but that was impossible. Joe Donovan was dead. Reputable sources confirmed his passing. She'd stood before his grave marker at Arlington. She'd mourned until her lifetime supply of tears had been spent. Every fact and circumstance underlined his death.

But she knew in her heart that the man who had kissed her was her husband. *Go with that. Go with him.* Clumsily, she unbuttoned her blouse and unfastened her belt. As she undressed, she folded her clothing and made a neat pile on the polished surface of the dresser. Being tidy with her clothes gave her a sense of control in a situation that was beyond comprehension.

Naked, she crawled between the smooth sheets. Her dizziness was gone, replaced by a firm resolve. A kiss had been her first clue. Making love would confirm his identity. She called to him. "Please come in."

The man who entered was Nolan Law. He was scarred. The bone structure of his face was heavy and rugged. His body was more muscular and well-developed than Joe's had ever been.

"Tess, I'm sorry if I upset you."

"Stop." She threw up her hand like a traffic cop. "No words."

"Okay."

"Make love to me."

He closed the door and turned out the light. A comforting darkness surrounded her. It occurred to her that she was asleep and this was only a dream. If so, she didn't want to wake up.

She heard him taking off his clothes. Zippers unzipped. His boots dropped to the floor, one by one. Without seeing him, she felt his presence as he lifted the covers and slid between the sheets.

And then he touched her.

His hand brushed her cheek. In a light stroke, he traced the line of her throat all the way down to the valley between her breasts. She remembered the first time they were naked together; he'd been so gentle and sensitive.

His lips trailed kisses along the path of his touch, and she felt herself coming to life. Her body had been dormant, but now her blood rushed. Sensation rippled across the surface of her skin. He hadn't forgotten how to excite her.

She reached for him, feeling him instead of seeing him. Her fingers explored the raised scars on his left side. His body was different, but she knew him intimately. She knew that he was ticklish on the right side, knew that he liked when she nibbled his earlobe.

A low groan rumbled through him. His rasping voice might be different from the clear tenor she remembered, but that feral growl was exactly the same. When it came to lovemaking, her Joe was a tiger. His gentleness was a teasing prelude to serious, ferocious passion. She knew what was coming next, and she couldn't wait.

The tempo of his kisses turned fierce. His hands were aggressive and demanding as he yanked her against him, taking her breath away. The full length of their bodies collided. Their legs entwined.

Reaching down, she grasped his erection. *Oh, yes, this was her Joe.* She giggled.

"What's so funny?" he whispered.

"If you'd been naked when we met, I would have known you in a minute."

"I've missed you so much."

"Don't tell me." She didn't want to talk, didn't want to think about anything but the sheer joy of being with him. "Show me."

"I don't have a condom."

As if that mattered? "What's the worst that could happen? That we'd create another Joey?"

"I'd like that."

She grabbed his chin and kissed him hard. "Make love to me now."

Swept away, she gave up any attempt at conscious thought. Each touch drove her higher. She clutched at him. He held her so tightly that she couldn't breathe. Her lungs throbbed. Muscles she hadn't used in a long time were aroused to action.

She heard herself crying out, demanding more.

His growling response sent wild shivers through her. She wanted him inside her, needed him. They joined in hard thrusts. Waves of pleasure rocked her body, rocked her world.

When she separated from him, she collapsed onto the pillows. Every cell in her body was vibrating. As slowly as a feather on the wind, she floated back to earth where she reveled in pure contentment.

He kissed her cheek. "Tess, I love you."

"Hush. Don't speak."

"Why do you keep telling me to be quiet?"

"Because…" She wanted to stay in this moment, clinging to this precious dream before she had to wake up and face the real world. "When I start talking, you're not going to like what I have to say."

"I know you're mad, and I don't blame you." He kissed her again. "You can't be angrier at me than I am at myself."

Oh, I doubt that. She pushed him away. "You were always impatient. Do I have to explain the difference between boys and girls? You might be energized, but I like to lie back for a few minutes and enjoy the ride."

"It was a good ride."

"The best."

She lay very still, trying to recapture the sensation of purely physical pleasure and deep relaxation. She and Joe had always been good together. Their sex life was more than satisfying. She and Joe… His name ricocheted inside her head. *Joe, Joe, Joe, where have you been? Why did you leave me?* She had to find out, but she wasn't ready to hear his story. And she damn sure wasn't ready to forgive him.

He fidgeted beside her on the bed and cleared his throat.

Before he could speak, she turned her back to him. "I don't want to get into this. Not now."

"We have to talk. Come on, Tess. I want to work things out."

"Just like that?"

He wasn't talking about a minor relationship issue like forgetting their anniversary. This was a five-year separation. He'd faked his own death. If he thought he could toss out a quick apology and expect her to forgive, he was clearly insane.

She sat up and snapped on the bedside lamp. For a moment, her anger was derailed by the sight of his thoroughly masculine body. His arms were huge. He had washboard abs. The scars and blotched skin from where he'd been burned didn't make him less appealing. Before he was injured, Joe had been nearly perfect. And that was how she still saw him. Perfectly infuriating.

"You broke my heart. I was in so much pain. You can't imagine what it was like. There were plenty of times when I didn't want to go on. If it hadn't been for Bart, I would have taken a swan dive off a tall building." The truth splashed in her face like a bucket of ice water. "Bart was in on this."

"He made it possible for me to die."

"You're not dead." She yanked up the sheets to cover her breasts. "Damn it, Joe."

Lying back on the pillows, he grinned. "You don't know how good it feels to hear you say my name, my real name."

"I wept at your grave. You had a hero's funeral. Oh my God, this is so wrong. Who the hell is really buried at Arlington?"

"That was arranged by Bart through the CIA."

"Isn't that fraud?" She hadn't even begun to consider the legal ramifications. "I'm receiving a widow's benefit. And an insurance payout."

"Bart, again," he said. "Those checks come through a trust he set up. I wanted to make sure you and Joey were well taken care of."

"While you played dead."

He winced. "When you put it like that—"

"How else could I put it? You let me think that you were dead. You weren't there for me. I was pregnant, Joe. Pregnant with your son, and I was a widow."

"Do you think I wanted that?" He sat up and confronted

her. "You're everything to me, Tess. The only way you and Joey would be safe was if I was dead."

She stared into his gray eyes, looking for the truth. He was sincere, but that didn't assuage her anger. She looked away from him as she pieced together the bits of the story he'd told her. "This is about Greenaway."

"The man who tried to kill you this morning," he said. "He's been watching, waiting for his revenge."

"But he still thinks you're dead."

"You're the only one who knows Joe Donovan is alive."

He reached toward her and glided the back of his hand along her cheek. His touch sent a little tremor through her, and she pulled away. She didn't want to be distracted.

"Five years ago in Afghanistan," she said, "you revealed Greenaway's plans to the CIA, even though you knew you were signing my death warrant."

"It wasn't like that. After I got hit by the IED, I didn't expect to survive. Greenaway had no reason to go after you if I was dead."

She understood that he'd been faced with a terrible choice: protecting her or doing what was right for his country. But there was so much that couldn't be explained. "When you knew that you were going to make it, why didn't you contact me?"

"I was pretty much out of it for a month. Bart told me that when I could talk, it was always about you. I wanted to get back to you, Tess. The reason I survived was for you and for my son."

"But you didn't come back."

"When I was finally coherent, Bart had already arranged for me to be dead. The deed was done. We didn't think Greenaway was interested in coming after you."

"And still," she said, "you didn't come back."

He looked away from her. "I was in no shape to protect

you. Never mind that my face looked like Frankenstein's monster, I couldn't walk. Hell, I could barely move."

Did he think she was so shallow that she would have rejected him? "I would have done whatever it took to be with you. I would have nursed you back to health."

"And you would have been in danger." He shook his head. "I couldn't do that to you."

"That should have been my decision." She hated that he and Bart had made their plans behind her back. "You lied to me."

"I'm sorry."

When he reached toward her again, she slapped his hand away. She wasn't ready to forgive, might never be able to forgive. Wrapping a sheet around her like a toga, she climbed off the bed, gathered her neat pile of clothes and stalked into the bathroom.

She hadn't decided where she was going or what she was going to do, but staying in bed with him was out of the question. Naked, she was vulnerable. Her body was already yearning for his touch, and she would not allow herself to be seduced.

Joe Donovan was a part of her life; they would always be connected. But she couldn't pick up where they left off and pretend that nothing had happened.

From the other room, she heard his cell phone ring. The sound annoyed her. He hadn't even muted the phone while they were making love, and that was rude. If she ever allowed him back into her life, there was a lot he needed to learn about relationships.

She came out of the bathroom while he was ending his call. He wore only his black boxers, and she had a clear view of his injured left leg. The scars were pretty horrific, and she understood what he meant when he said he wasn't expected to walk again.

She was so drawn to him. And so angry.

He held up the phone. "That was Coltrane. He located the guy Roxanne mentioned."

"Elliot."

"He was a janitor at the private school Victor went to. And he still lives near Bethesda. Coltrane found his house. He's waiting outside for me to join him."

"What about me?"

"I can arrange for Soarez to come here and pick you up."

That wasn't going to work for her. She refused to be shuffled out of the way. "I'm coming with you."

"Too dangerous."

"The way I see it, Greenaway could kill me whether I'm with Soarez or back at Pierpont House or anywhere else. You're not leaving me behind."

She was making the decisions, now. And it felt good.

Chapter Fifteen

He still thought of himself as Nolan Law. Even though Tess knew who he was, he hadn't earned the right to reclaim his identity as Joe Donovan. Joe died a hero. Nolan came back as a flawed survivor.

Tess hadn't spoken to him since they left the hotel suite. She was mad, and he couldn't blame her. It was bad enough that he'd put her through five years of mourning, but even worse was the deception. He'd lied to her, created an elaborate ruse. Clearly, he was at fault.

He accepted the regret and the shame. Yes, shame. Never before had he felt less than honorable. Nolan usually took the moral high ground, usually knew the difference between right and wrong. He was the kind of man who faced up to his responsibilities. But he had lied to the woman who was more important to him than life itself.

In the elevator, other people boarded, and the silence between them seemed less weighted. But as they walked through the parking garage under the hotel, the sound of their footsteps echoed. Though they walked side by side, they were alone, trapped by their own private agenda.

The only reason he kept walking instead of cutting his own damn throat was their lovemaking—the relevant word being love. She couldn't deny her visceral response to him.

The minute they starting kissing, they connected on a level that went deeper than her anger and his regret.

He got behind the wheel of the Hummer. Before he put the key in the ignition, he looked toward her. "It's not like you to use the silent treatment."

"I've changed," she said.

Not in any of the important ways. She was still gentle, caring and smart, but he wasn't going to argue. "Got it."

"But you're right. I'm not a child, and I won't act like one. I was quiet because I was considering the task at hand."

His natural inclination was to keep her out of the loop so she'd be safe. But he was done with deception. "What do you want to know?"

"How did Coltrane find Elliot so quickly? It's only been a couple of hours since we talked to Roxanne."

"We have a secret weapon at the CSaI offices, and her name is Amelia Bond. She's the office manager, but she does more than answer the phone and sort through files. When it comes to uncovering information, she's a genius."

"A computer expert?"

"An electronics wiz, and she also has a web of contacts. It's strange because she doesn't seem to have much of a social life. When she's not at work, I never see her."

"Sounds exotic," Tess said. "A woman of mystery."

"Amelia is the farthest thing from a femme fatale. She hides behind her glasses, wears baggy clothes."

"But she gets the job done."

"Without fail."

Tess raised an eyebrow. "Does Amelia know you're Joe Donovan?"

"No," he said with certainty. "When Bart was pulling strings and changing me into Nolan Law, he used his top secret clearance and called in a lot of favors from the CIA. For all practical purposes, there's no record."

The dim light in the garage came through the windshield and barely illuminated her face. Still, he noticed her tension. Her jaw clenched. Her brows pulled down and deepened the crinkles at the corners of her eyes.

"I don't know what to call you," she said.

"For now, I'm Nolan Law."

She nodded. "I won't be telling Joey. Not until we have things sorted out."

That hurt. After meeting his son, Nolan was eager to step up and become part of Joey's life. "I don't want to rush things."

"Again," she said, "not your decision. I know what's best for my son."

He started the engine and plugged the address Coltrane had given him into the GPS navigation system. At this time of night, the drive shouldn't take more than half an hour.

Tess asked, "Should we expect to find Elliot at home?"

"Coltrane has been watching the house. He has infrared, heat-sensing equipment." Nolan drove toward the garage exit. "That equipment is used for—"

"I know about infrared heat sensors. You can see through walls and get images of life forms inside." She shrugged. "I use them in a computer game."

"You play fantasy war games?"

"Joey wanted the game, and I got it to test and see if it was age appropriate, which it definitely wasn't. Way too violent for a four-year-old. But I kind of enjoy blasting my way through an army of zombies."

The image of lovely Tess with a blaster tickled him. She'd always had a sense of humor; it was one of the reasons he fell in love with her. "You're a good mom."

"Because I kill zombies?"

"You know why." She was responsible about what Joey should be exposed to, but she also was fun. "Anyway, Coltrane said there are two people in the house."

"Victor?"

"Probably not." It wouldn't be that easy to locate Victor. Bart's son had been clever enough to take on a new identity and evade discovery in the Middle East for years. He was good at staying under the radar. "I'm not a hundred percent sure Victor is even in this area."

"I thought you had a credible source," she said.

"Unfortunately, he was killed before he could give us details."

Jessop had told them that something big was going down. Victor, using his Wes Bradley alias, and Greenaway were going to be in Washington at the same time. From the start, Nolan hadn't liked the shape of that situation. If Victor was allied with Greenaway, Bart was in extreme danger.

He headed north following the navigational directions. The GPS voice programmed into the Hummer sounded like a staff sergeant he'd had in the Marines. He turned the volume low so he wouldn't snap to attention and salute.

For the most part, Bethesda was an upscale area—the kind of place where an exclusive private school would be located, but he didn't expect Elliot to be living in a mansion. The guy was a janitor at the school, not a rich preppie.

Tess said, "Victor is supposed to be highly intelligent, right?"

"Right," he said.

"If he happens to be in the house with Elliot, I think he'll notice a big white Hummer pulling up to the curb."

"Point taken. I'll park a couple of blocks away and walk closer."

"And what about me?" she asked.

"You stay with the car." As soon as he spoke, he knew that plan wouldn't fly. "But I can't leave you alone and unprotected."

"I have to come with you and Coltrane."

She sounded far too cheerful about the prospect of facing danger. Her attitude reeked with courage and initiative. It was exactly for those reasons that he'd known he couldn't tell her that he was still alive. Tess wouldn't have been content to arrange occasional clandestine meetings, nor would she be willing to give up her identity and hide in witness protection.

His wife looked like a delicate porcelain doll, but she was a scrapper, not afraid to fight for what she wanted. Taking on Greenaway and his network of distributors was beyond the scope of half a dozen government agencies. He and Tess didn't have a chance against them.

"I taught you how to use a gun," he said.

"Indeed, you did."

"Do you remember?"

"I don't go to target practice on a regular basis," she said. "But I've kept my skills up. I'm a single mom. I've had to protect Joey."

Drily, he said, "I wasn't aware that marksmanship was part of the single mom's handbook."

"Now you know our secret. Rabid dogs are nothing compared to a pack of single mothers. Threaten our kids, and we'll rip you to shreds."

Without another word, he took the gun from his ankle holster and handed it to her. From the corner of his eye, he watched as she checked the clip and balanced the heft of the automatic in her hand. Her competence was evident.

Tess might turn out to be the best partner he'd ever had.

At a bland one-story house in a neighborhood of similar structures, Tess prepared herself to approach. Their plan was simple. Coltrane would enter through the back door while she and Nolan came through the front.

Heat sensing images showed the two occupants of the house sitting side by side, probably watching television. The level of danger seemed negligible, but she still felt a rush of adrenaline through her veins. Taking action was a thousand times better than waiting to be attacked.

This morning when bullets were flying, she'd been nearly paralyzed by fear. And now? Not so much.

Her hands weren't shaking. She didn't feel faint. The opposite was true. She felt strong and fierce, as though she could take on the world. Was it because she knew Joe was alive and her period of mourning was over? Or was she so furious that there wasn't room for fear?

Either way, she was in control of herself as Nolan picked the lock at the front of the house and coordinated his move with Coltrane on the hands-free phone. They timed their entry, both coming through the door simultaneously. She followed Nolan, holding her automatic with both hands.

Though tempted to yell something like "on the floor, scumbag" or "die, zombie, die," she kept her mouth shut while Nolan and Coltrane subdued a man and a woman, using zip ties to handcuff them.

The two occupants of the house were an unattractive couple. Elliot had the kind of thin, dirty blond hair that always looked greasy. His shoulders were skinny and he had a potbelly. In spite of the winter chill, he wore a grungy sleeveless T-shirt that displayed the tattoos on his upper arms—several variations on skulls, daggers dripping blood, snakes and spiders. He didn't seem frightened by the assault. His eyes were close-set and mean.

His girlfriend was much younger, probably in her twenties. Her eyes were dull, nearly lifeless. Tess wondered if the girl was on drugs.

Coltrane did the questioning. Both Elliot and the girl were sitting cross-legged on the floor, and Coltrane loomed over them—big and threatening. Was this the same guy who played tea party with his twin girls? He had transformed from loving dad into harsh interrogator.

She knew that all the men in CSaI were former military. They had all seen combat. They were all trained experts. But seeing Coltrane and Nolan in action was a bit unsettling.

At first, Elliot played cute, pretending that he didn't know anybody named Victor. "I'm going to sue your ass," he said. "You can't bust into my house and push me around."

"Here's the deal," Coltrane said as he drew an eight-inch serrated blade from a sheath on his belt. "We're not cops. We don't have to follow the rules."

Nolan touched her arm. To Coltrane, he said, "I'll take the lady into another room. She shouldn't have to see what you're going to do."

As they moved into the hall, she whispered, "He isn't really going to do anything horrible with that knife, is he?"

"No, the threat is enough." He pointed her toward the end of the hallway. "Let's take a look around. See if we can find any evidence."

Throughout the house, the décor was decidedly weird. Busy patterns with flowers and swirls covered the curtains and furniture, reminding her of a design her grandma might like. But grandma would never abide such a mess. Dust spread across every surface. The carpets looked like they'd never been cleaned. One of the bedrooms was marginally cleaner with twin beds that were neatly made.

She stood at the foot of the beds. "It looks like they tried to tidy up in here."

"Victor might have been keeping Bart in this room." Nolan pointed to the pattern of wear on the carpet. "You can see how the beds were moved farther apart. Maybe that was to make room for Bart's wheelchair."

"Good observation. Do you think he left us a message?"

"Maybe." He dug into his back pocket and took out two pairs of disposable latex gloves. "Put these on. There's no point in leaving our fingerprints."

"Are you calling the police?"

"The CIA," he said. "Coltrane already notified Omar Harris. He ought to be here in ten or fifteen minutes."

Nolan circled the bed close to the inner wall of the room, studying the wall to see if Bart had managed to write a clue. He looked between the mattress and the box spring, felt along the floor. "Nothing. If Victor brought his father here, he did a thorough job of policing the evidence."

From the front room, she heard Coltrane growling his questions. The girl yelled at him. The screeching tone of her voice cut through Tess. She didn't like this part. "We should look in the other bedroom. I doubt that Elliot was as careful as Victor."

They picked through the mess in the bedroom. The stink of unwashed sheets rose from the bed. She hated to think of Bart being held captive in a disgusting place like this. The wicker trash can was full to overflowing. Breathing through her mouth so she wouldn't be hit with the smell of a rotting banana peel, Tess tipped the contents onto the carpet.

There were several amber vials—containers for pills.

She held one up so Nolan could see. "I don't know much about drugs."

He took it from her and read the prescription label. "It's a painkiller. I'm guessing that Elliot and his lady friend like to get high. Let's check these out."

All the vials came from the same pharmacy. The patient names were different. She asked, "Did they steal this stuff?"

"Stole it. Bought it. Who knows?"

She turned one of the vials over in her hand. "This one is from a different place. A drugstore in Freedom, Texas."

The patient name was B. Bellows.

Bart had been here.

Chapter Sixteen

Nolan returned to the room where Coltrane was still trying to extract information from Elliot and his girlfriend. He pulled Coltrane aside and showed him the prescription vial with Bart's name. The evidence was undeniable but didn't do them any good unless Elliot knew where Victor had gone next.

They needed to change the pace of their questioning. Coltrane had intimidated the hell out of Elliot and his girlfriend. Nolan would step in and supposedly offer them a way out.

He hunkered down so he was eye to eye with Elliot and showed him the prescription vial. "You're in serious trouble. This belongs to Bart Bellows. Do you know who he is?"

Elliot sneered. "Victor's old man."

"Bart was CIA. He's got friends in high places—friends in the CIA, friends in NSA. They're going to make you talk."

"I don't have to say anything. I know my rights."

"Let me tell you a little something." Nolan lowered his voice. "There are no lawyers at Gitmo. That's where you'll be headed. Think about it."

Nolan patted Elliot on the back and stood. When he'd entered the house, he'd left the front door standing open.

The December air had dropped the temperature in the house to an uncomfortable chill. Both Elliot and his gal pal were shivering.

Casually, Nolan sauntered to the door. Across the street, he saw Christmas lights twinkling on the eaves of a one-story bungalow that looked a lot like this one. The people who lived in that house might be a nice, normal family with a mom and dad and a couple of kids, maybe even a dog. Their biggest worry might be whether to have ham or turkey for Christmas dinner.

To Nolan, that seemed like heaven. A nice, normal life with no worries, it was all he wanted for himself and Tess and Joey. As he turned, he caught her gaze. The glimmer in her eyes didn't look like anger. It was a different kind of heat—at least that was what he told himself. He needed to believe that she was attracted to him. When he tried a grin, she turned away.

He closed the front door. When he came back toward their two prisoners, he took a knitted afghan from the sofa and draped it over the girl's shoulders. She had only a couple of girly tattoos of flowers and rainbows, nothing like the skull-and-dagger horror show on Elliot's upper arms. The only creepy one was a brown spider on her wrist just above the place where the zip tie fastened.

He pointed to it. "Is there a story behind this?"

Elliot warned her, "Don't tell him nothing."

Nolan noticed the same tattoo on Elliot. "Matching tats."

She looked up at him. Her pupils were dilated. Her lower lip quivered. "Elliot got the tattoo for me."

"Shut up," he yelled. "You dumb broad, shut up."

"Not so dumb," Nolan said. "Your girlfriend is getting smart. She's cooperating. She's not going to end up in Gitmo. Not like you."

"You can't—"

"Not me," Nolan said. "I'm a nice guy. But these other feds, they can make you disappear. Understand?"

"I get it," Elliot grumbled.

"What do you want? It's your choice."

"Don't turn me over to the CIA. I'll cooperate. But this still isn't right. I didn't do nothing wrong."

At the minimum, Elliot had harbored a fugitive and aided in a kidnapping. "You're ready to talk. That's good."

"Why should I take the fall for Victor? He's rich, had everything handed to him on a silver platter."

"I'll get back to you," Nolan said. "First, I want to hear what the lady says about her tattoo. I've seen spiders like that. It's got a marking on the back that looks like a violin. We used to call them fiddlebacks."

"It's a brown recluse spider," she said.

Like the Recluse Gang. The boarding school boys had chosen a moniker that referenced a spider known for powerful venom. Cute, real cute. "Are you part of the gang?"

"Honorary member," she said. "There were only eight of them, you know. Like eight legs on a spider."

"Do you know their names?"

She shook her head. "Just Elliot and Victor."

"Did you meet Victor's father? His name is Bart."

"I wasn't supposed to have anything to do with him," she said. "But one time, I sneaked into the room. He was sleeping."

"Is that when you took the vial of painkillers?"

"There were only two pills left," she said. "I threw the bottle away so nobody would know."

That explained how Victor had overlooked such an incriminating piece of evidence. He hadn't paid enough attention to Elliot's addict girlfriend.

There was one more question Nolan needed to ask. "Have you ever heard the name Greenaway?"

She thought for a few seconds and then shook her head. "Nope."

He turned to Elliot. "How about you?"

"I got to explain something to you," he said. "You're wrong about Victor. He's taking real good care of his dad."

Nolan covered his disgust and disbelief with a tight smile. Victor had abducted his father. He'd set a bomb in a day care and had murdered Bart's driver. There was nothing sympathetic or righteous about his actions. "Tell me about Greenaway."

"I know he's a bad dude. If I ever hear him getting close, I should run."

"Was Victor in touch with Greenaway?"

"Not a chance. He was hiding from him."

That wasn't the story Nolan had expected. If Victor hadn't come to D.C. to meet with Greenaway, why the hell was he here? "Do you know how to get in touch with Victor?"

"I never did," Elliot said. "Over the years, he'd just show up on my doorstep. He'd stay for an hour or a week. I never knew how long. He'd leave me some cash, and then—poof! He was gone."

Nolan had heard enough. He stepped away from Elliot and his girlfriend and pulled Coltrane aside. Standing near the front door, they conferred.

"You got a lot out of them," Coltrane said.

"After you softened them up. I'm not sure how much we can believe. Did you contact Omar Harris?"

Coltrane nodded. "He'll be here soon. We should talk to Harris about the rest of the Recluse Gang. Victor might be staying with one of the others."

"And get Amelia on it."

"You think she'll have better luck than the CIA?"

"I wouldn't be surprised," Nolan said. "I'll leave you to it. I should take Tess back to the Pierpont House."

Coltrane grinned. "How's it going with you two?"

He wasn't sure how to answer that question. The other guys in CSaI didn't know his real identity, but they were sharp enough to know that he was hiding something in his past. Someday, he hoped to tell the truth, to reclaim the life he'd lost. But not yet.

"I like Tess. A lot."

"You've got my blessing," Coltrane glanced at her and winked. "I was real surprised when I saw her come running in here with a gun. There's some depth to your little party planner."

Nolan signaled to her, and she quickly joined them.

"What's next?" she asked.

"I'll take it from here," Coltrane said. "You should get some sleep. Tomorrow could be a big day."

"It absolutely is a big day. There's the caterer and the printer and the florist and the Alamo cake."

Nolan added, "Not to mention saving Bart's life."

"Sorry." She cringed. "My priorities are out of whack."

"You're thinking of everything. That's good." He reached toward her, then thought better of the gesture and tucked his hand in his pocket. "Either way, we need sleep."

He opened the door for her, and they retraced their steps back to the Hummer. The night air was bracing but not invigorating enough to jump-start his brain. Though he wanted to start a real conversation with her, the right words seemed out of reach.

"The weatherman says no snow for Christmas," he said.

"Global warming," she mumbled.

"I wouldn't mind a nice day in the seventies."

She stopped short and tilted her head to look up at him.

The glow from a streetlamp burnished her hair. "You don't have to force a conversation. I'm accustomed to long silences."

"Because I disappeared, right?"

"Because you died." Her lips thinned into a hard, straight line. "There's a significant difference. Dead means never coming back. Oh, wait! That's not what it means at all."

"I get it, Tess."

"I don't think you do. It's clear that you've been operating at your peak, running CSaI. Did you even think about me?"

"Every hour of every day."

She started walking again, walking fast. He kept pace beside her. He could have told her about the pain—physical and emotional. And he could have apologized. Again.

Instead, he went quiet. She was right. It was his fault they'd been separated. Nothing he did or said would change the facts.

Inside the car, she exhaled a long sigh as she fastened her seat belt. "I'll try to stop sniping at you. It's just that I'm having a hard time pretending that everything is normal."

"We have a lot to discuss. Should we go back to the hotel?"

"In your dreams."

"Never hurts to try." He started the car. "I'll take you back to Pierpont House."

"Thank you." She checked her wristwatch. "It's coming up on midnight. I should be exhausted, but I'm not. It feels like I'm bouncing around in a pinball machine with bells ringing and lights flashing."

He remembered, "Like the pinball machine in that retro

tavern we visited when we were on vacation in the Bahamas."

"That was fun, but not what I was thinking about. I have a computer game that plays pinball."

"First the zombie-killer and now pinball, you're quite the little gamer."

"It gives me something to do late at night when I can't sleep." She shrugged. "Why am I so lit up?"

"You're reacting to the action we took earlier, something to do with how adrenaline floods your body. I can't explain, but I know what you're talking about. Time gets weird. You look at your watch, thinking only a minute has passed, but it's an hour. Or the opposite happens and time stands still. Either way, your brain won't turn off."

"That's a fairly good description."

"You used to meditate," he said. "That might help."

"That's a great idea. I should have thought of it."

"You're lucky to have me around to remind you."

"Uh-huh," she said, "we'll see about that."

He watched as she adjusted the seat and wiggled into a comfortable position. She closed her eyes. He could see the tension leaving her neck and shoulders. Her hands rested limply in her lap. Her chest rose and fell at a steady pace.

A long time ago, she'd told him about her two-minute meditations where she imagined a distant horizon and allowed her mind to sink into a pure, white calm. He'd tried to follow her instructions, sitting in a yoga pose on the floor in their bedroom. But he could never get beyond the blue sea and the horizon.

Instead of fading to blank, his imagination created surfers and sailboats. Then the sharks would show up. Enlightenment wasn't his thing. He was ever alert to the dangers below the surface. *You relax. You die.*

He checked the rearview mirrors to make sure they

weren't being followed. After that first assault at the Pierpont House this morning, he hadn't seen anything that would hint at assassins. It probably didn't hurt that Omar Harris and his men had paid a visit to the Zamir household. No arrests had been made. The suspicious nephew had disappeared as had a black SUV registered to him.

Nolan seriously doubted that the Zamirs would be hiring Donovan Event Planning in the near future. Tess wouldn't be happy about the loss of business, but it was a small price when you considered that the Zamirs had tried to kill her.

Her meditation had slipped into slumber. Her head lolled to the side. Her lips parted, and she made a snuffling noise. She'd always snored a bit, even though she denied it. He liked her little sleeping sounds. Her flaws made her special; knowing those flaws made her his woman.

In the area approaching Pierpont House, he parked at a curb. The most dangerous point of their journey was the arrival when he had to slow down to enter the gate. He took out his cell phone and called ahead to make sure the gate was already open and he wouldn't have to slow down.

Beside him, Tess stirred. It seemed a shame to disturb her, but she'd wanted to get back here.

He unfastened his seat belt and leaned toward her. There were a number of ways he could have awakened her. Jostling her arm or calling her name. But he chose to steal a kiss.

Gently, he joined his lips with hers. She wiggled a bit as he increased the pressure. Her mouth was soft and sweet. He stroked his fingers through her silky hair.

She gasped, and then she kissed him back. Her arm encircled him, pulling him closer, holding him tightly. She deepened the kiss. Her tongue pushed against his lips, and he drew her inside his mouth.

Passion roared through him, the same fierce passion that he'd felt in the hotel suite. His hand tangled with the seat belt as he reached for her breast.

She pulled back. "What are you doing?"

"Waking you up. We're almost to the Pierpont House."

"I can't believe we're making out in the car like a couple of horny teenagers."

He glanced toward the back of the Hummer. "It's a big car. We could get comfortable in here."

She gazed up at him. For a moment, he actually thought she might be considering his proposition, and his heart soared.

"No," she said firmly. "What happened earlier tonight isn't going to happen again. Not until I decide what to do."

"Keeping that resolution won't be easy. Tess, I can't keep my hands off you."

"That's your problem," she snapped.

"Is it?" He caressed her cheek. "You kissed me back."

"I won't let that happen again."

Next time, he hoped, she'd kiss him first.

Chapter Seventeen

The next morning, Tess awoke to another kiss. Joey had come upstairs to the bedroom at Pierpont House and crawled into the bed beside her. "Wake up, Mommy."

"Hey, kiddo."

She snuggled him close but didn't open her eyes, not wanting to leave a wonderful dream of Joe. She mentally corrected herself. *His name is Nolan.* She didn't want to slip up and call him by the wrong name. Joe or Nolan, it didn't matter. He was alive in her heart, and she couldn't stop thinking about him.

But how could she ever trust him? He'd lied to her for five years. No decent relationship was possible without basic trust. Not even if the sex was incredible. Her dreams had been one replay after another on a continuous, fabulous loop. Her body was still tingling and moist. If she kept thinking like this, she'd never get out of bed. And that would not do.

Pushing Nolan out of her head, she opened her eyes and looked at her son. "How was your campout last night?"

"We had marshmallows. And we had a fire in the fireplace, but we didn't have to get twigs."

"Because the fireplace is electric," she said.

"Can we get a fireplace for our house? Can we? Please."

She didn't know if Joey consciously asked questions

when she wasn't really awake, but she'd noticed that his most outrageous requests generally came before she got out of bed. More than the usual pleading for a dog, he'd ask for a snake that ate mice or just the mice or if he could write his name on the wall with fingernail polish. His early morning creative endeavors knew no boundaries.

"No fireplace," she said. "Next summer, we can go camping and build a real fire in the forest."

"In a real tent?"

She immediately pictured Nolan camping with them, showing his son the ways of the wilderness. Joey could learn how to fish and whittle a stick and skip rocks across a lake—all those things that fathers and sons did together. They'd both love it. How could she deny them that relationship?

Rolling onto her side, she turned away from the light that crept around the edges of the window. "Mommy needs more sleep."

"It's late," he said. "I already had breakfast."

With a groan, she squinted at her wristwatch. It was after eight. She had to get up and get moving. There were a million things to do before the Smithsonian event tomorrow. "You're right, Joey. I'm up."

"Can I come with you today?"

This request wasn't outrageous but a little odd. He usually hated coming along on her appointments where he had to be on best behavior. "It's not going to be interesting. I'm just doing business."

His eyes—so similar to his father's—looked up at her as though searching. He held her hand. "I won't be bored. I promise."

Her son couldn't possibly know what had transpired between her and Nolan; that secret was locked in a vault. Yesterday, she'd talked to the others in the house, and they had decided that no one would mention the possibility of danger to him. But Joey seemed to sense that something was wrong.

"Not this morning," she said. "I'm going to see a grumpy caterer named Pierre. He's no fun at all."

"I wanna come."

Later, she had an appointment at the Smithsonian to check out the blueprints with Nolan. "Maybe this afternoon, we can go to a museum. I'm not sure. But maybe."

Joey applauded and gave her another hug.

She hoped it would be possible to make good on that offer.

LESS THAN AN HOUR later, she was in the Hummer with Matt Soarez on her way to the caterer. Her handsome, macho bodyguard talked about how much his life had changed since he joined CSaI and married Faith.

He grinned when he said the name of his new wife, who was back in Freedom with her baby girl. Tess clearly remembered the rosy glow of newlywed happiness when everything was clear sailing. She'd crashed and burned since then. Was there really a chance to rise from the ashes?

Nolan hadn't been at the house this morning, and she missed seeing him. When she'd gotten dressed, she'd selected a soft pink turtleneck because he liked her in pastels. And she'd dabbed a bit of his favorite perfume lightly behind her ear. If he kissed her, he'd catch the scent.

Though she told herself that she was still too angry to be excited about seeing him, she was lying. She wanted Nolan to notice her, to compliment her. She longed to see his nod of approval and to hear his smoky-voiced compliments.

Trying to sound nonchalant, she asked, "Was Nolan planning to meet us?"

"I'm not sure. I know he'll be with you this afternoon at the Smithsonian."

And that appointment brought up another question. "Do you think it's safe for me to bring Joey to the museum?"

"The situation is changing minute by minute." Soarez gave a philosophical shrug. "The last I heard, the CIA was still looking for the young man you met at the Zamir house."

"His name was Ben."

"He's the real threat, and he appears to be acting without the knowledge of the rest of the family. Mr. Zamir is cooperating and hiding behind diplomatic immunity. His wife and daughter have moved to their Manhattan penthouse."

"I guess that means I won't be planning their dinner event next month."

"I wouldn't count on it."

Though the connection between Greenaway and the Zamirs was vague, she would never work with them again. How could she? Their supposed friends had tried to kill her.

She wasn't accustomed to thinking this way. The only issues that should concern an event planner had to do with table decorations and, of course, the food.

IN THE PARKING LOT outside the catering service, Nolan and Coltrane were waiting. The two tall, rugged men leaned against the hood of a black Mercedes sedan. Since the weather today was cool but sunny, their dark glasses didn't seem odd.

Nolan had his arms folded across his chest. She saw the hint of a smile when the Hummer approached—a smile that was meant for her. Automatically, she smiled back. Her heart did a backflip.

He opened her car door and took her hand to help her climb out of the Hummer. "Good morning, Tess. Sleep well?"

His sly grin suggested that he'd been able to read her mind and knew all about her sexy nighttime fantasies. She was slightly breathless as she replied, "I slept well. And you?"

His voice was so low that only she could hear. "I couldn't help feeling that something was missing from my bed."

That would be me. Aware that the others were watching, she took a backward step. "Why are you all here? You can't be interested in the banquet food."

Nolan answered, "Coltrane and I came to get a list of all kitchen staff and servers who will be at the event. We need to do background checks."

"This catering service has security clearance. That's one of the reasons the Smithsonian likes to work with them." Avoiding Nolan's gaze, she asked Coltrane, "Couldn't you have just called for the list?"

"We could have," Coltrane said, "but we find that people are more cooperative when we meet them in person."

"I understand." She looked from him to Nolan. "I've seen you in action. You're very...persuasive."

A green Volkswagen bug zipped into a parking place, and Trudy hopped out. Her gray-haired assistant bustled closer. She stopped and frankly stared at the three men from CSaI. Her blue eyes twinkled. "Is it just me or is it hot today?"

As Tess introduced her, Trudy took her time, flirting with both Coltrane and Soarez. When she came to Nolan, she reached up and patted his cheek. "I certainly remember you, young man. I understand you and Tess have been spending some time together."

"Yes, ma'am."

"You'd better treat her right or you'll answer to me."

"Wouldn't have it any other way," he said.

Before Trudy could launch into a discussion of dating rules, Tess called a halt. "Let's all go inside, shall we?"

As Tess dug into her briefcase for her notes, Trudy joined her. She was beaming. "I haven't seen so much testosterone in one place since we did that dinner for the Navy SEALS."

"You're shameless," Tess said.

"You can't blame me. I mean, look at those boys. Especially Nolan."

"Can we focus on this meeting?"

"Oh my," Trudy said. "You slept with him."

Was it that obvious? Tess swallowed hard. "Why would you possibly think that?"

"I might be old, but I'm not dead. I can tell when a woman has that well-loved glow." She sniffed the air. "And you're wearing perfume. I know what's going on with you two. And it's about time."

"We'll talk about this later."

Tess strode to the door where the three sexy bodyguards were waiting. Without making eye contact, she entered the front office of the catering firm. The walls were hung with various wedding photos. Poinsettias lined the walls. Inside the glass-topped counter were menus in fancy script and various place settings.

The three manly men looked somewhat out of place, and the female facilitator seemed eager to make them comfortable. She dashed from her desk to greet them and fell all over herself to assure Coltrane that she would get those lists immediately.

Because Trudy had been in touch with the florist, the ice sculptor and the cake baker, she stayed at the front to work out a few details for the event. The main issue was timing. Governor Lockhart's event started at six o'clock, earlier than usual for this type of dinner. And Santa Claus would arrive at half past six with gifts for the children.

Tess guided Nolan and Soarez through a swinging door into the industrial-size kitchen, where four workers in white chef coats were busily chopping at their stations. The savory scent of roasting fowl floated through the air.

Pierre, clad in a black chef jacket with the sleeves rolled up, stalked toward them. He glared at his Patek Philippe wristwatch as if to indicate that they were wasting his time. Every time she met with the chef, he found something new to complain about.

After she did the introductions, Soarez firmly shook the chef's hand. "I'm looking forward to your partridge in a pear tree appetizer. Nice choice for Christmas."

"A brilliant choice." Pierre didn't hesitate to toot his own horn. "I considered doing the entire menu from the 'Twelve Days of Christmas' song with French hens and goose eggs. But the 'seven swans a-swimming' weren't practical for a large dinner party."

Tess had heard this idea before and had vetoed it. She wouldn't put it past Pierre to slaughter the "eight maids a-milking." She asked, "Did you get my message about the additional twenty-six guests?"

"Seven of them children," he grumbled. "Why are there so many children at this event?"

Much as she hated to point out the obvious, she said, "It's Christmas Eve. Parents want to be with their kids."

"Which is also why we're eating at such an absurdly early hour," he said. "Six o'clock."

Nolan spoke up. "Look on the bright side, Chef. Kids are easy to feed."

"Perhaps for someone like Tess. She can just throw another hot dog on the grill."

Spoken like a man who was childless. She prided herself on feeding Joey fresh veggies and healthy grains, but she wasn't about to get into an argument with the chef before a big event. "Is everything on track? If you have any special needs, now would be the time to tell me."

"My people will be on site at four-thirty. Ask me then."

She'd been hoping to avoid last-minute hassles on Christmas Eve, when a lot of suppliers wouldn't be open, but the chef didn't seem to care about the calendar. "I'll be there after lunch," she said. "The museum closes at one tomorrow, so the florist shouldn't have any problem setting up."

"Very well." He waved a hand, dismissing her. And then, he turned to Soarez. "You, my friend, are in luck. We're practicing the partridge appetizer. I insist that you taste."

"I'd be honored."

Pierre swept through his kitchen like a king, ordering his minions who jumped to do his bidding. If his staff wasn't actually afraid of him, they put on a pretty good show. She wondered how many sous-chefs Pierre fired in an average month.

Walking beside her, Nolan murmured, "This guy's a diva."

"You are so right."

Not all great chefs had huge egos, but Pierre was definitely over the top. He spread a sheet of butcher paper on a chopping block and set a plate in front of them.

"Designed to be finger food," he said, "I present a

confit of partridge with walnuts and poached pear in a pastry shell."

The presentation was visually appealing—garnished on top with a tiny slice of pear and a mint leaf. She picked up the small pastry and took a bite. The flavors were unusual but delicious.

Apparently, Soarez and Nolan agreed. Both had finished their pieces and were making yummy noises.

Before she could take her second bite, the tender pastry shell crumbled. Rather than drop her partridge on the floor, she shoved the whole thing in her mouth. She felt globs of pear sauce smearing her face.

"As I feared," Pierre said, "the pastry is too fragile."

"Not for me," Soarez said.

"Men eat in one bite. Women in two. I'll use decorative paper cups so the ladies won't spill on their gowns. This was useful, Tess."

"Happy to help," she said.

"You've got some stuck over here," Nolan said as he reached toward her. With his thumb, he brushed the crumbs from her chin. The intimate gesture seemed perfectly natural until she looked toward Pierre and saw him scowl.

"I see," said the chef. "Is this your boyfriend?"

There was no point in denying the truth. "I suppose he is."

Pierre rested his hand on his chest. "Madam, you break my heart."

Chapter Eighteen

After turning the list of catering employees over to a CIA analyst and emailing a copy to Amelia, Nolan headed back to Pierpont House. It was noon and everybody—from the governor to the twins—was sitting down for lunch. The long dining room table was a scene of organized chaos with a half-dozen conversations and food being passed in both directions.

After a couple of quick hellos, his gaze went to Tess. As soon as he looked at her, the rest of the world faded into the background. She excused herself from the table and came toward him. "I have to ask you a question," she said.

"Ask me anything."

She nodded toward Joey. "In private."

"Even better."

He gestured, and she followed him down the hallway to the small office with a window that looked out on the parking area. As he closed the door, he watched her cross the room. Her soft pink turtleneck was tucked into gray slacks that hugged her bottom. She was more slender now than when they first met. Her waist was tiny, but she still had curves. It took all his willpower not to pull her into his arms for a long, deep kiss.

Though he hadn't made a move, she must have guessed

his intention because she circled the desk, putting distance between them. "I told Joey that he might be able to come to the museum with us this afternoon. Is it safe?"

The idea of an outing with his wife and son sounded so blessedly normal that he wanted to sing. His first instinct was to say yes, but he hadn't spent the past five years in hiding to get careless now. "Omar tells me that the CIA is closing in on Greenaway's location."

"Will they be able to stop the weapons deal?"

"I hope so. The products to be exchanged include five ground-to-air missile launchers. Sophisticated weaponry, those babies can be hoisted on a shoulder and can shoot a chopper or a plane out of the sky."

"My God," she whispered.

Finally, she was beginning to understand the scope of the threat. When it came to illegal arms and opium, they didn't get much bigger than Greenaway. "Coming after us is a secondary concern for him. Right now, Greenaway is busy protecting his own ass."

She took a breath to calm herself. "Does that mean the museum trip is on?"

Nolan mentally ran through the precautions that were already in place. They'd take the bulletproof Hummer and park in the private garage under the museum, which was itself a well-secured building. Plus he'd be with them as an armed bodyguard. Joey would probably be safer than if he was on a preschool field trip. "We can pull this off."

"I'm glad," she said. "Joey really wanted to be with me today. I think he's sensing that there's something wrong."

"And he wants to protect you."

Her gaze met his. "In that way, he's kind of like you."

"You think so?" Pride swelled in his chest. "You think Joey inherited my instincts?"

"You don't have to look so pleased," she said. "I'm the

one who's going to be raising a fearless kid who's ready to take on the world. My life would be easier if he was timid."

Not my boy. He came around to her side of the desk. "Our trip to the caterer was interesting."

"The partridge appetizer was tasty."

"And how long has Pierre had a crush on you?"

"He doesn't," she said firmly. "I don't know what that broken heart comment was all about, but it had nothing to do with the way he feels about me."

"That's not what Trudy says."

"Yeah, right. Trudy thinks that every man who says hello is madly in love with me. She's the queen of wishful thinking."

He thought Trudy was probably correct. Men were interested in Tess, but she chose to ignore them. "Trudy said that Pierre keeps showing up at your office for no particular reason."

"It's strictly business. Pierre never asked me out, never made a pass. If he's attracted to anybody, it's Soarez."

Nolan smirked at the idea of macho Soarez and the French egomaniac. "Yeah?"

"Soarez asked a couple of questions about breakfast menus his wife could use at her café, and Pierre thought he was a fan. He gave Soarez a cookbook with twenty different omelet recipes."

"There's only one omelet I really like—three different kinds of cheese, spinach and asparagus."

When they were married, she'd made that omelet for him on lazy Sunday mornings when they lingered in bed. They fed each other bites while they read the newspaper. He knew she was remembering the same thing. Her smile was wistful as she said, "I like that, too."

It occurred to him that talking about food might be the way to her heart. "What else do you like?"

"Simple flavors, done to perfection."

He leaned a little closer and lowered his voice. "I thought you were more of a gourmet."

"There's not really much difference between fancy and plain. It's just a matter of how you describe the food," she said. "That's something I've learned as an event planner. I can make anything sound exotic."

"Give me an example."

"Our sauce today uses organic eggs from free-range Nantucket hens whisked and emulsified with safflower oil and the juice of a Eureka lemon. *Voilà!*" She brought her fingertips to her lips to kiss the imagined taste. "That, my friend, is a description of mayonnaise."

"I love mayonnaise."

"I know you do."

He asked, "What do you love?"

Her expression softened. For a second, he thought she was going to tell him that she loved him. Instead, she turned her back and went toward the window. "We can't do this."

"A friendly chat about breakfast? What's the harm in that?"

"We're too grown up and we've been through too much to play games," she said. "I'm attracted to you. That goes without saying. But I don't want it to go too far."

"Too late," he said.

"I don't regret making love to you. For years, I dreamed about your kisses and the feel of your hands on my body. I never wanted anything more. But there's more to life than what happens in the bedroom."

Her voice trembled at the edge of tears. He didn't want

to upset her. "It's okay. We can go as slow as you want. I won't push."

Her shoulders stiffened. When she spoke again, she was in control. "I lost you once, and it nearly killed me. I can't bear to lose you again."

"You won't."

"That's a promise you can't make." Abruptly, she pivoted and faced him. Her eyes were clear, and her voice was steady. "You're a soldier. You're not an active marine, anymore. But you're not the kind of man who would run away from a fight. Being in CSaI is just as dangerous as being in combat."

"I can change jobs." He would do anything for her. "I could go back to school and study computers or accounting. If you want, I can work as a CPA."

"Even then, you'd find a way to make it dangerous. That's who you are. That's the man I married."

"You loved me then."

"That was before I had a child. My life is different now. I want stability, not risk."

He understood what she was saying, but he didn't buy it. The world was a big, mean, scary place. She and Joey were a lot better off with a man who would fight for them. No matter what it took, he'd keep them safe.

"Tess, I'm only asking one thing. Keep an open mind."

"Fine." She gave a quick nod. "I'll tell Joey we're going to the museum."

AT THE NATIONAL Museum of American History, Tess introduced Nolan, Coltrane and Omar to the events planner and left them to study the blueprints while she spent time with Joey. She needed a break and was content to leave security concerns to the experts.

Their first stop was the 26,000-square-foot transportation hall on the first floor that showed the progression from horse-and-buggy to present day. This wasn't Joey's first trip to a museum. Last spring, they'd gone with her mom to the National Air and Space Museum. He'd been fascinated by the cool stuff, but he had no interest in hearing any informative details.

On this trip, he was better behaved and more focused—able to stand still for more than thirty seconds at a time. His maturity pleased her and made her sad at the same time. Her little boy was growing up.

He listened while she read the information about the 1903 Winston—the first car driven all the way across the country. She pointed to the statue of a white dog. "That's Bud, the first dog to ride all the way across the country."

"He's got glasses," Joey said.

"Those are goggles to protect his eyes."

Joey stuck his neck forward, "Hello, Bud."

Then he laughed, took her hand and tugged. A good-size crowd was meandering through the exhibits. Schools were on vacation, and many businesses took time off this near Christmas. That meant finding something to do with children who were already hyperexcited about Santa Claus' imminent arrival. She and Joey rolled with the flow as they checked out the trolley car, the old-fashioned orange school bus and the massive Southern Railway locomotive.

On one level, she was enjoying herself, but her tension hadn't dissipated. She found herself checking out faces in the crowd. Surely, the bad guys couldn't get in here. There were metal detectors and museum guards. Still, she was watching, looking for danger.

When she spotted Nolan coming toward her, she was relieved. He'd never let anyone hurt them. And that was part of the problem. A brave man steps into the line of fire.

Nolan wouldn't hesitate to take risks, and she couldn't live with the very real possibility of losing him again.

The smart thing would be to shut this door and walk away, but it wasn't that easy. When he smiled at her across the museum, her pulse raced. More and more, she was seeing Joe in him.

Joey charged toward him, and Nolan lifted the boy in his arms. The ease and naturalness of the gesture tugged at her heart. Father and son were together again.

Omar was with him, wearing a nondescript suit with a Santa necktie. She gave him a smile and introduced her son.

Joey shook his hand. "Pleased to meet you."

"Same here," Omar said.

Joey announced, "We're done in here. What's next?"

"I'd like to go upstairs," she said, "to the area where the event will be held."

Without hesitation, Nolan directed them to the elevator. Having spent some time studying the blueprints, he must have memorized the layout of the museum. On the second floor, he escorted Joey through the Flag Hall to the Star-Spangled Banner, leaving her alone with Omar.

He cleared his throat, "Nolan asked me to bring you up to date on our investigation. There are things you should know about the Recluse Gang."

She raised an eyebrow. "Is this something we can talk about in public?"

"It's not top secret. Not secret at all," he said. "There was nothing special about these high school misfits until they banded together and started making up their own rules. They claimed they drank blood. They were involved with drugs. And they all got spider tats."

"That must have caused a stir," she said. "I'm sure an elite boarding school didn't allow tattoos."

"Which is why they chose their symbol carefully. The spider was brown and small, barely noticeable. Victor had one. His medical records from the Army mention the tat on his wrist."

"They burned down a building, right?"

"The explosion in the science lab was supposed to be a prank on the teacher who gave Victor a failing grade, but it got out of hand and caused serious damage. They were all expelled, and Elliot, who was a janitor at the school, got fired."

"How many in the gang?"

"Eight," he said.

She remembered, "That was what Elliot's girlfriend said. Like the eight legs on a spider."

"Five students, Elliot, a local drug dealer and a teacher."

Last night, their concern had been to find another of the Recluses who might have offered another place for Victor to hide with Bart. "Where are they now?"

"Three of them got their acts together and are successful businessmen. None live in this area. The teacher was killed in a car accident. Another of the kids is dead. The drug dealer is in jail."

"So this is another dead end," she said. "Is investigating always like this? Following a bunch of leads that never reach a destination?"

"It's all about interpreting what we've got. The original Recluse Gang doesn't provide any suspects, but there might be others. Elliot saw fit to have his girlfriend get the tattoo, and I doubt he's smart enough to think of that all by himself. I wouldn't be surprised if Victor recruited others to his cause."

"His cause?" She was disgusted. "It seems like all he believes in is revenge."

"Bottom line," he said, "you should be on the lookout for anybody with a spider tattoo on the wrist."

"Are you any closer to finding Bart?"

"If Victor wanted his father dead, he would have already killed him. Instead, it appears that he's taking care of Bart, keeping him doped up but still tending to his needs."

On the far side of the spacious hall, she saw Nolan and Joey walking hand in hand. Joey had a bounce in his step and was chattering happily while Nolan listened. *Her boys.* They were adorable.

No matter what she decided for herself, Tess would never deprive Joey of a relationship with his father. They needed to be together.

When she looked over at Omar, she realized he was watching her. Like Bart, he was CIA—privy to information no one else knew. Was he aware that Joe Donovan and Nolan Law were the same person? "How much do you know about Nolan's past?"

"He's a hero and a good man. There's nothing else I have to say."

She interpreted his statement as a way of telling her that if he knew about Nolan, he wasn't talking. "Do you mind if I ask you a personal question?"

"You can ask." His grin was friendly but his dark eyes were less than encouraging.

"It must hard for men like you and Nolan to have a stable family life. How do you manage?"

Omar chuckled. "I can't believe you're asking me for relationship advice. I'm on my third marriage."

"But it sounds like you're happy." She remembered their conversation in the Minuteman Café. "You have a baby. You're looking for the best schools for her to attend."

"My wife doesn't like what I do for a living. My job requires long absences, and I can't tell her what I'm doing or where I am. None of my wives liked being married to an agent. But it's who I am." He shrugged. "The only thing I can tell you, Tess, is that it takes a special kind of woman to be with a man whose life involves a certain amount of danger."

She gazed toward Nolan and Joey. There was no denying the love she felt for them. But was she that special kind of woman? She wasn't sure.

Chapter Nineteen

That night at Pierpont House, Nolan put his son to bed at nine o'clock. For most dads, this was no big deal. For him, these moments were precious. He couldn't have been happier when Joey asked for a story.

Standing behind him, Tess said, "Nothing violent, okay?"

"That pretty much rules out the Grimm brothers."

"Maybe a story about the museum," she suggested.

Nolan sat on the edge of his son's bed. "Once upon a time, there was a dog named Joey."

"Hey, that's my name. Was he a border collie?"

Nolan nodded. "Just like the dog that lives near me in Texas. And Joey the dog went to the museum to see Bud, the first dog to ride across the whole country."

Nolan kept talking about the museum and the two dogs roaming through the exhibits looking for a bone until Joey's eyelids drooped. Within minutes, his son was asleep, breathing steadily.

Leaning down, Nolan kissed Joey's warm forehead. This was the best, the absolute best. No way in hell would he be separated from his family. Not again. Not ever.

The only problem was convincing Tess to take a risk on him. In the hall outside the bedroom, she waited for him. Her eyes were moist but her lips curved in a poignant smile. "That was a great story," she said quietly. "Have I told you that I really like your raspy voice?"

"I'm not a pure tenor anymore. Throat damage."

"It's sexy."

He took the cue, leaning down for a slow, lingering kiss. Her arms climbed his chest and wrapped around his neck. Her body pressed against him. She was kissing him with a lot of enthusiasm. Convincing her that he was worth the trouble might not be as hard as he'd thought.

He held her lightly, cupping her breast. As soon as they made contact, he was aroused. He wanted to carry her to the nearest bed and make love to her.

"Not here," she whispered. "There's no privacy in this house."

"Come back to the hotel with me."

"Oh, that sounds good." She licked her lips. "But I should stay here tonight in case Joey wakes up. I need a good sleep. The big event is tomorrow."

Since he'd promised not to push, he backed off. But he wasn't ready to leave her. "How about if we go downstairs and have a cup of tea?"

"Is this like a date?"

"It's whatever you want to call it."

They descended the back staircase that opened into the kitchen. Of course, there were other people around. This was a big place, but the governor and her entourage had filled every available area.

While they made their tea, he engaged in standard conversation, but his focus was Tess. With their tea in mugs, they wandered down the hallway and ended up in the office, again. This time, she didn't dodge him and hide behind the desk. They sat side by side on the sofa.

"Tomorrow," he said, "I want you to be very cautious. Don't go anywhere alone."

"The Smithsonian ought to be safe."

"It should be. But I got another piece of information from Omar that worries me. It's about the break-in at your house. The CIA forensics people found a fingerprint."

"I'd almost forgotten about the intruder and having all my things pawed through. I guess that says something about how much has been happening over the past few days." She stared into her teacup and frowned. "Who was it?"

"The print belonged to Victor."

"I don't understand." She looked up at him. "Is Victor working with Greenaway?"

He didn't have a thorough explanation. He'd been turning this information over in his mind ever since Omar told him. "Victor and Greenaway have had dealings in the past. Victor might have come to D.C. as part of a weapons deal, but it's doubtful that they're currently working together."

"Why not?"

"Bart is Greenaway's enemy. And it's pretty clear that Victor is taking care of his father. He doesn't intend to turn Bart over to Greenaway."

She set her teacup on the coffee table and leaned against the back. "I've never met Victor. What could he possibly have against me?"

"I don't know." He'd really tried to make sense of it. Why ransack Tess's house? "If Elliot can be believed, Victor is on some kind of revenge mission. Your only connection to him is through Bart. Is there something Bart might have given you that he was after?"

"I didn't really have time to look around and see if anything was missing, and I can't think of what he might take. Bart has given me a couple of very nice presents, but I doubt that Victor would go after my industrial-strength juicer. I don't keep valuables in the house."

She hesitated, and he guessed that she had something more to say. "No valuables at all?"

"They aren't related to Bart."

"You're holding back." He turned her face toward him. "Don't make me guess."

"My engagement ring and your Purple Heart. I keep them in my bedside table."

A gentle warmth spread through him. Her two most precious things were from him—one signified their life together, the other came from his death. He loved this woman so much.

He took her hand and squeezed. He wanted to kiss her, but he feared that if he started he wouldn't be able to stop. "Tomorrow, I'll check with Omar and make sure those things are still there."

"It doesn't make sense for him to touch those things."

"Here's the problem with Victor." He remembered his conversation with Dr. Leigh. "It's likely that he's suffered from bipolar disorder for most of his life, and he hasn't received treatment."

"How could a serious illness like that go undiagnosed?"

Several incidents should have acted as signposts, starting with the cruel pranks Victor played when he was only a kid. In high school, his Recluse Gang burned down a building. He and Elliot attacked Roxanne. In Iraq, he nearly beat a man to death and was well on his way to a dishonorable discharge. "Someone should have noticed."

"But they didn't."

"At this point, the CIA profilers suggest that he's having a psychotic break that makes him hard to read, as complicated as a Chinese puzzle box. His logic won't make sense to you or me."

"It's very sad. I almost feel sorry for Victor."

Her voice was soft and sweet as a spring breeze. The

whole time they'd been apart, he had imagined her voice, but his fantasies were nowhere near as pleasing as hearing her speak. He could listen to her for hours.

There was only one other voice that echoed in his mind—a voice he'd heard long ago. He would never forget Greenaway and the threats he'd made in the still Afghan night and at the moment when Nolan should have died. That audio memory was branded into his mind. The voice of a devil.

And Tess was an angel.

"Whether or not you pity Victor," he said, "he's dangerous. I want you to be alert. He's got a grudge against you."

"Understood."

"There's something else I want to do. To keep you and Joey safe," he said. "Tomorrow after the event, I want you to come back to Texas with me."

"You've got to be joking. Tomorrow is Christmas Eve. It's going to be impossible to get plane reservations."

"Not if you're flying on Lila Lockhart's private jet."

Her eyes widened, and then she grinned. "If I turned down a ride on a private jet, my son would kill me. Yes, Nolan, we'll fly away with you."

He couldn't have been happier.

THE NEXT AFTERNOON, Tess left early to oversee final preparations. Nolan felt safe enough to drive the Mercedes; the bulletproof Hummer would be needed later to transport the kids. At the rear of the building, they waited to clear security with the Smithsonian guards. Then he drove into the underground parking reserved for dignitaries and special deliveries. The catering trucks would also use this area for unloading. Instead of parking, Nolan drove around the perimeter.

"Where are we going?" she asked.

"I want to see if the reality matches the blueprints. There's another floor under this one that's used to store exhibits that aren't on display. Any doors connecting with that level are locked." He switched his dark glasses for his horn rims and pointed to a dark metal door in the shadowy corner. "Like that one."

"And why is this information important?"

"Basic security," he said. "In case of emergency, we need to know all the possible exits and entrances. The only access between floors is the freight elevator and the doors that connect with the lower level café."

"You know, it's a shame this parking lot isn't open to the public."

"Too risky. The artifacts in this building make it a potential target."

"For what? Terrorists who want to steal the ball gowns that belonged to the first ladies?"

"You'd be surprised." He drove back toward the freight elevator.

Her adrenaline was pumping. She was feeling antsy and couldn't wait to get started. "This is my favorite part of event planning."

"Why is that?" he asked.

"For weeks, I've been putting together all these details and now I get to see the end result. It makes me think of a symphony when the instruments finish warming up and join together." A thought popped into her head. "Which reminds me, I need to make sure the string quartet knows how to play 'The Yellow Rose of Texas.'"

He found a parking space near the stairwell. "Let me know if I can help."

The last thing she needed was big, muscular Nolan messing with her centerpieces. "You just make sure the security is in place. The event coordinator told me that they wouldn't have as many guards as usual because of the holiday."

"CSaI is on it." He reached into his suit coat pocket and took out a small plastic object with a clip on the back. "I want you to wear this so I can stay in contact."

She turned the bit of plastic over in her hand. "Does this let me hear everything you say and vice versa?"

"That's right."

"Sorry, that doesn't work for me. I have my own headset that I'll be using to communicate with Trudy and Stacy. If I hear too many voices in my head, I'll go crazy."

He took the piece and adjusted it. "Now it's just one-way. I can hear you, but you won't hear me."

"The stuff I'm doing is going to bore you," she warned. "Detailed discussions about flowers and folding napkins."

"My darling," he said with a grin, "you'll never bore me. Just clip it onto your bra strap and forget about it."

"Why do you need to hear me?"

"There's going to be a lot going on. I won't be able to keep an eye on you all the time and that worries me. I can't do my job if I'm obsessing about you."

In a weird way, his obsession was a compliment. She attached the device to her bra. "Happy?"

"I would have been happier if you'd let me put it on."

As she got out of the car, she grabbed the garment bag with her gown. They took the basement staircase beside the freight elevator to the second floor. The museum had just closed, and the last visitors were being herded toward the exit.

Tess left her gown in the office of the event coordinator—a brisk, business-oriented woman who told her that she'd be here in her office if she was needed.

"I'll let you know," Tess said.

"We're shorthanded," she said. "I wanted to let as many people as possible go home for Christmas Eve. Tomorrow is the only day of the year that we're closed."

"I understand."

Outside the office, she and Nolan parted ways. He had security concerns, and she had a high-class dinner for over three hundred people. Though she carried an electronic notebook filled with information, the details were embedded in her head. She positioned herself in the second floor Flag Hall where a soaring ceiling rose above the huge metallic abstract of the Star-Spangled Banner. The real thing—the actual flag from Fort McHenry that inspired Francis Scott Key—was housed in a temperature-controlled display case in an adjoining area.

The tables and podium were quickly assembled and draped with red tablecloths. Trudy arrived with the florist who had worked with Tess before and did not disappoint. The festive centerpieces used yellow roses and white lilies highlighted with deep green pine branches and candles.

For the next couple of hours, Tess hustled from place to place. She added signage downstairs at the front entrance where the museum had already done holiday displays appropriate to several cultures, including a Christmas tree, a menorah and Kwanzaa candles and drum. Back on the second floor, she checked the microphones. On the lower level, she helped the baker who delivered the spectacular four-foot-tall Alamo cake. The ice sculpture—a map of Texas with a cowboy and a longhorn—would come at the last minute.

After Tess carefully placed the name cards on the tables, she checked her wristwatch. It was almost four-thirty. The caterers would be arriving. She didn't want to get into her party clothes too early, but there wouldn't be time later. She slipped into the office of the event coordinator where she'd hung her dress.

Stacy greeted her. "Everything looks great, Tess."

"Especially you." Stacy's floor-length, sleeveless gold dress with a scoop neck set off the warm tones in her complexion. Her brown hair hung in graceful curls to her shoulders. "That's a beautiful gown."

"This old thing?" Stacy twirled. "Actually, I've only worn it once before. I love the long skirt because I don't feel bad about wearing comfortable shoes under it."

High-heeled shoes were the bane of Tess's existence as an event planner. She never put them on until the last moment. Until then, it was ballet flats all the way. "I hate to make you mess up your hair, but I need you to wear a headset so we can communicate without yelling."

"Got it." Stacy took the microphone headset. "Who else is on the line?"

"Just you, me and Trudy."

"I'll be at the front with the guest list. Is there anything else I can do?"

"We're on schedule," Tess assured her. "I'm going to get dressed, and then check on the caterer."

As she dressed and used the private bathroom to touch up her makeup, she thought about Pierre. The last time she'd seen him, he'd made that odd comment about his broken heart. Did he really have a crush on her? Hard to believe but stranger things had happened. Tonight, she'd be sure to coddle him like a newborn chick. A negative mood from the chef could affect the whole event.

She smoothed her hair into a sleek, high ponytail so it would look neat and not get in the way, then she put on her headset. After one more glance in the mirror, she decided that the emerald silk dress was nearly perfect. The bodice was similar to a long-sleeved shirt dress with a plunging neckline and ruffles. The matching belt made her waist look small. Her outfit was dressy without being over-the-top, and the color was appropriate for Christmas.

As she left the office, she almost ran smack into Nolan. He caught her by the arms, holding her in one place. His gaze slowly caressed her body from head to toe.

"Beautiful," he murmured.

"Thanks." She basked in his approval. It felt good to have a man notice how she looked. From the day they first met, he'd been attentive to those details. "And what are you doing here?"

"Your mic was quiet. I got worried."

"I was getting dressed, but I remembered to put it back on." She inclined her head toward her bra strap. "Can you hear me now?"

"Loud and clear." He grinned. "I have some good news. Omar called. The CIA is moving on Greenaway tonight. This could be over real soon."

It was too much to believe. She and Joey would no longer be under threat. The danger that had kept her husband away from her for five years might be eliminated. There would be no physical reason for them to live apart.

Chapter Twenty

Taking Greenaway out of the picture didn't mean an end to all their relationship problems, but Tess considered it to be a very good start. If they didn't have to ride around in bulletproof Hummers worrying about sniper attacks, she and Nolan could actually confront their personal issues.

Now wasn't the time to think about anything but the event. "Keep me posted."

"You really are beautiful," he repeated. "I'm not just talking about the dress. You have a glow, an energy. You enjoy this work, don't you?"

"It suits me."

"I like seeing you in your element, doing a job that makes you happy. I'm guessing that you're good at event planning."

"Well, I'd hold off on the praise until after I've dealt with Pierre and his crew." She reached up and patted his cheek before she took off. "Wish me luck."

"Always."

She rode the elevator down to the lower level, where the catering staff was already unloading their trucks into the kitchen for final preparation. These caterers had worked other events at the Smithsonian so they didn't require directions. Pierre stalked among them, issuing instructions and quick reprimands. Some items would go directly to the staging area near the service area on the second floor. Others needed to be cooked or reheated.

Having worked as a caterer herself, Tess recognized a smooth, professional operation. She wouldn't interrupt the flow of activity, but she wanted Pierre to be aware that she was available if he ran into any problems. Before she could catch up to him, he was in the service elevator.

As the doors closed, she was fairly sure that he saw her and quickly looked away. Now what? Was he avoiding her? She tamped down her irritation and took the stairs.

Over her headset, she heard Trudy arguing with the string quartet. Tess stopped in the Flag Hall to put out the fire. By the time she got into the staging area for the food, Pierre was gone. Under her breath, she muttered, "I don't have time to play cat and mouse."

Stacy responded, "What's that about mice?"

"It's nothing," Trudy answered for her. "Tess talks to herself sometimes. I try to ignore it."

Tess checked her wristwatch. There was less than an hour before the doors opened. "Would you ladies keep an eye on things for ten minutes? I need to catch Pierre. I'll be out of communication until I find him."

She turned off her headset and hustled downstairs. In the kitchen, she spotted Pierre's heavy shoulders in his white chef coat and made a beeline toward him. Before he could disappear again, she caught his arm.

He whipped around and stared at her. His face was red, and he was sweating. "What do you want?"

"I'm sure you have everything under control. I'm just checking to see if there's anything I can do." He looked like his head was about to explode. "Are you all right?"

He gestured. "Come with me."

She followed him across the kitchen into the stairwell. The metal door closed. Pierre paced on the small landing.

He banged his fist on the metal railing. "I can't do it. I've worked too hard."

His eyes were red-rimmed as though he'd been sobbing. Unlike his usual tirades, these emotions seemed real and profound. Concerned, she said, "Tell me. I'll help you."

"You have no idea." He leaned his back against the concrete wall. With his left hand, he rubbed hard at his forehead as though trying to wipe off a deep stain.

For the first time, she saw him without his expansive gold watch. On his left wrist was a small tattoo—a brown spider.

The CIA analysts and Amelia had missed this connection. Pierre LeBrune was a member of the Recluse Gang. Tess touched the communication device fastened to her bra strap. She needed to say something that would alert him to this new threat. What would he tell her to do? *If you see a spider tattoo, run.*

Easing backward a step, she reached for the doorknob.

A sob exploded through Pierre's lips. "I owe everything to him. My life. My career. He never asked for anything in return…until now."

The knob twisted in her hand. Before she could open it, Pierre flung out his arm. He held the door shut. His voice was a whisper. "It breaks my heart to hurt you, Tess. You're a kind woman. I tried to tell him."

"Listen to me, Pierre. We can't hide in this stairwell forever." *Please, Nolan, please hear me.* "There's security all over this building. If you hurt me, you won't get away with this. You'll go to jail."

"If I betray him—" another sob interrupted "—Victor will kill me."

Pierre was a powerfully built man. It wouldn't take much for him to overpower her. Her only defense was words. "You can't let Victor tell you what to do. He's a sick man. He needs help. You could help him, save him."

"I wanted to tell you. I kept coming by your place so I could tell you. But I was afraid."

She heard a loud click as an outer door to the stairwell opened. Footsteps clattered on the concrete stairs. Someone was coming. It had to be Nolan.

She called out, "Help me. Hurry."

It wasn't him. The man who climbed the stairs was big and heavyset. He held a gun in each hand. He raised his arm and fired.

The shot echoed like thunder. Pierre gasped and clutched at his chest. Blood stained his white chef's jacket before he crumbled.

"Well, Tess, what's it going to be?" He gestured with the second gun. "This is a stun gun. It won't kill you, but I promise that it hurts a lot."

"You're Victor Bellows."

"Bravo, you're a genius. Let's hope you make the right choice. You can come along quietly or I can zap you."

She looked down at Pierre. He groaned. He wasn't dead. She couldn't help him or herself if she was unconscious. She threw up her hands. "Don't shoot."

"Bart told me you were a smart girl."

"Do you have Bart? Is he here?"

"This way. We're going downstairs."

Her lip trembled as she looked down at Pierre. She hoped Nolan would get here in time to help him. And to help her.

"Hurry," Victor snarled. "Don't tick me off."

She did as he ordered, going down the staircase until she stood beside him. "Is Bart all right?"

"My daddy is a strong old man. He'd be the first to tell

you." He reached toward her and snatched her headset. "Are you talking to Nolan on this?"

"It's to communicate with my staff."

He tossed the headset into a corner, opened the lower door and grabbed her arm to drag her through to the storage level. They went down a hallway to the right.

She tried to be smart, to alert Nolan to their whereabouts. "Where are you taking me? This level is all storage."

"It's a rat's maze. A maze for rodents." He talked in fast, staccato bursts. "Twists and turns that double back on each other and double back again. I went to a lot of trouble to get you and Bart alone."

"You used Pierre. He got you past the security guards and gave you access to the Smithsonian."

"Pierre, Pierre, that's not his real name, but it's good for a super chef. He earned it, didn't he? Didn't he?"

"Yes," she responded. Her instincts told her to agree with everything he said. She couldn't take a chance on upsetting him.

"The Recluse Gang." Victor laughed. "We were naive punks, but we were smarter than the teachers and our parents. When we got kicked out of school, Pierre had a serious cocaine habit. His dad kicked him out of the house. Pierre was pathetic. Pathetic Pierre."

He whirled around and faced her. His pale blue eyes stared with piercing intensity. "Do you know what my dad did? What the saintly Bart Bellows did when his little boy got expelled from that fancy ass school? He shoved me into the army. It was supposed to make a man of me. That's crap. He sent me away because he couldn't stand the sight of me."

She wanted to tell him that Bart loved him, but it

wouldn't be safe to contradict him. Instead, she tried to shift his focus. "In high school, what happened to Pierre?"

"I took care of him. Me, that's right, I did it. I take care of my friends. Pierre changed his name, never talked to his parents again and they assumed he was dead. That's what they wanted. They wanted him dead."

"But you didn't."

"I helped him, financed him, got him on his feet. With all I did for him, you'd think the guy could pay me back. Right? Yeah, of course, right. Instead, he grew a conscience. He felt sorry for you. Aw, poor Tess, the sad widow woman. You can see why I had to shoot Pierre's cowardly ass. No other way."

"Why are you so angry at me? I don't even know you."

"Unlucky for you, Mrs. Donovan. You were in the wrong place with the wrong guy. Or should I say, the wrong husband?"

"I don't know what you're talking about."

He shoved her so hard against the wall that her teeth rattled. "Don't be cute. Your husband is Joe Donovan. A war hero. A man who came back from certain death. Honorable. Admirable. I hate him."

NOLAN FELT LIKE he'd been training all his life for this mission. He had the preparation, the skills and the instincts to rescue Tess. Failure wasn't an option.

Activity pertaining to the banquet had gone into high gear, but his focus was elsewhere. Through the communication equipment that connected the CSaI team, he alerted them to Victor's presence. "He's got Tess. And says he's got Bart."

He arrived at the stairwell at the same time as Coltrane and Soarez. Weapons drawn, they entered the door to the first floor landing. At the lower level, they found Pierre. He was still breathing.

"Get him out of here," Nolan said, "and get him an ambulance. Don't let anybody else come into the stairwell. Not until I know what's going on."

Through the device he'd given Tess, he listened to Victor's fierce ramblings. Talking so fast that his thoughts couldn't keep up with his brain, he sounded like he was on speed. His stated hatred for Joe Donovan didn't make sense, unless it was somehow connected to Greenaway.

Nolan disregarded everything but the directions. At the stairwell, he should go right, then to the end of the hall and left. Visualizing the blueprints he'd studied earlier helped keep the setup in mind.

Coltrane came back into the stairwell and stood beside him, waiting for instructions. After this was over, all the CSaI guys would know his real story. It would be a relief to reclaim his identity.

He heard Victor repeat the directions. Something was wrong with this picture. Why would he be so specific? Then he heard his name.

"Nolan Law," Victor said, "I know you're listening. You wouldn't let Tess out of your sight unless you could track her."

Tess spoke up, "What are you saying?"

"Don't lie to me," Victor said. "I hate liars, and I know you've got a listening bug to stay in touch with him. Are you going to hand it over or should I search you for it? I wouldn't mind patting you down. You're a good-looking woman."

Nolan muttered, "Give it to him, Tess."

He heard her say, "Take it."

"Good girl," Victor said. "Here's the deal, Nolan. You have my location. I'm here with Tess and Bart. You've got five minutes to get here. Come alone or Tess pays the price. You got that, hero? Come alone."

The bug went dead.

Nolan looked to Coltrane. "Victor set up an ambush. He wants me there in five minutes. Supposedly, there's only one way in. But I remember the blueprints."

Quickly, he sketched out other routes to reach the area where he expected to find Victor. He was putting his life and that of Tess and Bart in the hands of the men he worked with. He couldn't ask for a better team. "Coltrane, you're in charge. Don't let me down."

"I've got your back. Stall him for as long as you can."

Nolan whipped down the last flight of stairs and emerged into the storage basement under the museum. He measured his steps carefully in case Victor had booby trapped the approach. It seemed doubtful that he'd want to stop Nolan. The revenge Victor was planning required his presence.

Through the communication device in his ear, he heard Coltrane mobilizing the other men. Four guys from CSaI—McKenna, Soarez, Coltrane and McClain—were enough to take on a regiment. Were they enough to handle Victor Bellows?

He paused before the last turn and pulled himself together. More than anything, he couldn't let his emotions get the best of him. He stepped into an open area with a concrete floor. To his right was a solid wall with doors. Floor-to-ceiling rows of shelves covered the rest of the space. Wooden crates and cardboard boxes with labels filled the shelves.

Directly in front of him was Bart in his wheelchair. Tess was beside him, about three feet away. Her wrists were fastened to the arms of a wooden chair with zip ties.

Victor held a titanium assault rifle to her head. In the dim light, her face was ashen, but her gaze held steady.

"About time you got here," Victor said. "Drop your weapon."

Nolan did as he said. Without prompting, he also removed his ankle gun. He was disarmed, except for a spring-loaded pocket knife that wouldn't do much good unless he got close enough to use it.

In a casual tone, he asked, "How are you doing, Bart?"

"I'm well. My son has taken good care of me."

"Damn right." Victor separated himself from Tess and kicked the discarded weapons out of reach. He pointed the rifle at Nolan's chest and frankly stared. "You don't look as bad as I thought you would. I heard your face got blown off."

"Who'd you hear that from? Greenaway?"

"Your nemesis," Victor said. "He scared the pants off you, didn't he? Not me. I dealt with him, face-to-face. Less than a week ago, I messed with the big, bad Greenaway. How about that, huh? Who's the tough guy now?"

His chest thrust out. Victor postured and posed as though he was the star of his own private movie. The longer Nolan could keep him talking, the more time his team would have to get through the locked exits and reach them.

"You're tough," Nolan said. "You survived a hell of a lot in Iraq and Afghanistan. That took guts."

"But you got the medal." He reached into his pocket and pulled out the case containing his Purple Heart.

"You stole that," Tess said. "You broke into my house and stole that medal."

"Calm down, cutie pie. I went to your house because was looking for you. But you weren't there. So I had som fun. Finding this piece of meaningless junk was a bonus.

"Not meaningless," she said.

"Your hubby isn't so brave. I'm the one who faced Greenaway. I outsmarted him."

"Why?" Nolan asked.

"Because Greenaway was after my father, and I decided that dear old daddy should live. I'm the guy who makes those decisions. Life and death, life and death, I hold fate in my hands. This hand…"

He lifted his hand above his head, then lowered it and pointed at Nolan. "Who dies? You?" Victor swung around. "Or Tess, your pretty little widow. Either way, death is coming. Tonight, somebody dies."

Nolan prayed that Coltrane would get here in time.

Chapter Twenty-One

"That's enough," Bart said quietly. "Victor, that's enough."

Tess pinched her lips together to keep from screaming. They could die, all three of them. Victor said that he'd gone to a lot of trouble to arrange this situation; she knew it wasn't going to turn out well.

She made eye contact with Nolan. For once, he wasn't wearing glasses. The strength in his gray eyes reassured her, as did his courage. No matter the cost to himself, he'd come to protect her and Bart. The man couldn't help being heroic. *That's who he is. And I love him.*

Victor was wary. He watched Nolan and kept a safe distance as he paced frenetically, circling between her and Bart.

"Please, Victor," Bart said.

"Don't tell me what to do, old man."

"I'm your father."

"When it suits you." Victor launched into a fast-talking diatribe. "You didn't want much to do with me when I was a kid. I was a pain in the ass, a problem, an inconvenience. After mom died, you couldn't wait to hand me off to a nanny while you went about your life, having adventures, leaving me behind with the likes of Roxanne."

"I loved you," Bart said. "I wasn't good at parenting, but I did the best I could."

"Yeah? Yeah?" Victor's voice went higher and higher. "Let's ask Tess about good parenting."

She felt Victor's hand on her shoulder. He tightened his grip, digging his fingers into her flesh. The pain cut through her fear. She couldn't just sit here, waiting for him to kill her. She had to do something.

Victor leaned down and whispered in her ear. "What do you think of a father who ignores his son? Who can't be bothered to take part in his only child's life?"

"Leave her alone," Nolan said.

"That cuts a little close to home, doesn't it?" Victor stood up straight and released his grip. "Good old Nolan, here. He wasn't even there for the birth of his kid. He missed out. Didn't see little Joey take his first step or say his first word. He didn't show up for birthdays."

Tess said, "It wasn't his choice. He was protecting us by staying away."

"That's what he told you. But is it true?" Victor crowed. "Face it, Tess, you and I got shafted. These heroes—these two big, fat heroes—are lousy fathers. I want my revenge. How about you?"

"No," she said quietly. "I can forgive."

"Wrong answer, sweetheart." He shoved at the back of her chair and it rocked on the wooden legs. "Mr. Purple Heart ought to explain this to you. When a man has a gun, like me, you damn well better agree with every word he says."

"Not when you're wrong," she answered.

He yelled in her face. "Have you got a death wish?"

"Hey." Nolan took a step toward them. "She doesn't know what she's saying. Victor, look at me."

"I'm looking, and I'm telling you this. If you take one more step, I'll shoot out your kneecap. Remember how much that hurts? It was your left leg that got blown to hell. I'll make the right leg match."

"I'm not defending him," Tess said. "My husband made mistakes. And so did your father. Bart might not have given you enough love and understanding. He might have been too hard on you, expected too much from you."

Victor whirled back toward her. "Now you're getting it. Keep talking."

"Bart Bellows is a legend in the CIA. He's known as a hard man." She hoped Bart would forgive her for what she was saying. If they survived, she'd apologize. "Maybe he just didn't have the love to give."

From behind Nolan, she heard a clattering noise.

Victor reacted. "What's that? Your buddies coming to the rescue?"

"I came alone," Nolan said. "Just like you said."

"There's only one way into this area. All the other doors are sealed." Victor braced the titanium assault rifle on his hip. "If they peek around that corner, they're dead."

"Stop it," Bart said loudly. "I'm the one you're mad at, Victor. And I don't blame you. I was a lousy dad and didn't do right by you. Kill me and get it over with. Let these other people go."

"You still don't get it," Victor said. "I don't want to kill you."

Tess believed him. If his goal had been to murder his father, he could have done it when he first kidnapped him. Victor's idea of revenge was more complicated.

He paced in a figure eight around Bart's wheelchair and her chair. "For a long time, I told myself that you weren't capable of love. Then I heard about CSaI. Your plan was to help men returning from war. You started with Joe Donovan. Gave him a new name, got him the best medical care you even took care of his wife and son."

His voice trailed away as he spewed incomprehensible gibberish. He was near the breaking point, losing touch with reality, dangerous.

She noticed that Nolan had moved closer. His muscles coiled. He was ready to strike, waiting for the right moment. Is she could create a distraction, they might have a chance.

With stark clarity, Victor said, "You took a broken man, Joe Donovan, and you made him into a hero. Nolan Law became the son you never thought you had."

He stood between Tess and Bart, staring at his father. "There's only one thing I wanted from you. Only one damn thing. I needed for you to be proud of me."

"It's not too late," Bart said. "We can start over."

"That's right. I'll take Nolan's place after I've killed him. When he's dead, I'll be your son."

Tess twisted her torso to the left. With all her strength, she hurled herself to the right. The chair toppled and hit Victor in the back of his legs.

He staggered and fell against Bart's wheelchair. The old man grabbed at the barrel of the gun. For a few seconds, they struggled. Victor regained control of his weapon, but he wasn't quick enough.

Nolan was on him. He threw a right jab. A direct hit. Victor's head snapped back, but he kept his hold on his gun. He fired without taking aim.

On the floor, Tess struggled to get up. She couldn't clearly see what was happening, but she was aware that the other guys from CSaI had appeared from the shelves behind them.

They yelled for Victor to stop, but he kept squeezing the trigger. Stray bullets flew in random directions.

She saw Victor go stiff. He dropped to one knee. Though he'd been shot, he wouldn't go down. Nolan ripped the gun away from him and came to her. "Are you all right?"

She nodded. "What about Victor?"

He glanced over his shoulder. "Soarez has him."

Using his pocketknife, Nolan cut the zip ties that fastened her wrists to the arms of the chair. "That thing you did by crashing into him," he said, "that was a risk."

"If you'd done something like that, I'd be mad." With her hands free, she reached for him. "But I'd forgive you. I'll always forgive you."

He helped her to her feet, and she wrapped her arms around him. The other four CSaI guys were watching, but she didn't care. She kissed him on the lips. He was her man, and she never wanted to be away from him again.

"Coltrane," Bart said, "call the paramedics."

"Are you hurt?"

"Not me," Bart said. "Victor was shot in the leg. He's in need of medical attention."

And Victor was still his son. Bart hadn't been the world's greatest dad. He'd made mistakes, the worst of which was not recognizing the symptoms of his son's mental disorder. And Victor had done a great deal of evil. But the connection between them could not be denied.

She snuggled against Nolan's broad chest, accepting the warmth that flowed between them. Their marriage was a bond that had been stretched thin but had not broken.

Chapter Twenty-Two

After answering questions from law enforcement, Nolan dragged Tess away from the Smithsonian. She'd wanted to stay and make sure Lila's event went according to plan, but he had convinced her—with help from Trudy and Stacy—that having her life threatened was a good enough reason to take the rest of the night off.

On the short drive from the Smithsonian to the hotel, she'd been on the phone with Trudy, running through the lists of tasks she carried inside her head. When he escorted her into his hotel suite, he took the cell phone from her hand. "Should I order room service?"

"Wine," she said. "I'd like a lot of wine."

"You're in luck." He'd left a bottle in the mini-fridge below the wet bar.

She cast off her coat and flung herself onto the sofa with her arms spread wide and her feet stretched out in front of her. "I should have stayed and done my job. But how could I? My sleeve is torn and the dress is ruined."

"I liked that dress." He pulled the cork from the wine bottle. "I'll buy you a new one just like it."

"Joey was okay, wasn't he?"

"You talked to him. What did you think?"

"He told me he was fine." A ragged sigh pushed through her lips. "Everything is kind of a blur."

He could tell that she was a lot more traumatized than she was letting on. Dealing with threats from a crazy man was enough to shake anybody. Nolan's job for the rest of the night would be taking care of Tess.

"Joey's doing all right. He got his present from Santa and he has plenty of other kids to play with."

"He said he wanted to stay at the Smithsonian." She couldn't help worrying after all they'd been through. "He'll be safe there, won't he?"

"A hundred percent safe. He wouldn't want you to be upset. He's a good kid."

"Brave like his father."

"Smart like his mother."

He poured the wine and placed the glass in her hand. She took a long gulp and exhaled another sigh. "This event was a total disaster. I'll never work in this town again."

"It's not that bad."

"Oh, but it is. The catering chef was shot and nearly killed. There was a shoot-out in the basement. The police and the CIA were all over the place. And before we left, I noticed that the ice sculpture was melting. The cow had lost its horns."

"In Texas, that cow is called a longhorn steer."

"Whatever."

He sat beside her. "The Alamo cake was pretty amazing."

For a moment, they sat quietly, sipping their wine. It was a comfortable silence—the kind of peace shared by people who understood each other and who loved each other. This would have been a perfect happy ending, except for one thing. Nolan still hadn't heard from Omar about the task force pursuing Greenaway.

She finished off her wine with a flourish and stood. "What time does the private jet leave for Texas?"

"Whenever we get there," he said. "They'll wait for us."

"I'm going to take a shower and change into my comfortable clothes." She reached down to stroke his cheek. "I wouldn't mind if you joined me."

"That's the best offer I've had in a long time."

"Let's rock and roll." Her lips curved in a smile.

"I need to make a phone call first."

She winked. "I'll be waiting. Naked."

He watched her walk into the bedroom. Even with a torn sleeve, that green dress was something special—classy and beautiful, just like his wife. After tonight, he felt justified in claiming that relationship. Though not without problems, they were husband and wife.

Unbuttoning his shirt, he took out his cell phone and called Omar on his private cell phone. When he answered, Nolan said, "I couldn't wait. What happened?"

"This is one hell of a task force. We've got law enforcement from half a dozen different agencies. The good news is that we picked up several of Greenaway's men, including the guy connected to the Zamirs. We confiscated all the weaponry, except for one ground-to-air missile launcher."

Nolan guessed the bad news. "Greenaway got away."

"He's on the run, but he's not going to get far. We've closed down all the escape routes out of Washington. We'll get him. Don't worry."

Nolan took off his jacket and draped it over the back of a chair. He could hear the water from the shower starting. "Let me know what happens."

"From what I've heard, you had some excitement at the Smithsonian. How's Bart?"

"Tough as ever."

"You take care of that old man. He's been talking to a lot of people, calling in favors, making arrangements.

There are some people who don't like the way he plays fast and loose with the law."

"That sounds like a warning, Omar."

"I hope there's no cause for concern. Just keep an eye on him."

"Easier said than done." Nolan disconnected the call.

Bart was a force of nature, larger than life. He'd had a month of forced inactivity while he was kidnapped to make plans. Now he had launched his strategy for taking care of Victor with ferocious energy.

Nolan took off his shoulder holster and pulled out his shirttail, baring his chest. He entered the bedroom. Tess had left the door to the bathroom open, and steam billowed toward him. She was waiting for him, naked in the shower mist.

He'd only taken one step into the room when he heard the door to the suite being opened. In an instant, his gun was in his hand. He braced himself.

Bart called out, "Everybody decent?"

Unfortunately, yes. Nolan put down his weapon and greeted Bart and Soarez, who pushed the wheelchair into the suite.

"We won't stay long." Bart glanced around the room and nodded. "I've always liked this hotel. They've got everything I need, including a helipad on the roof."

"Excuse me," Nolan said as he entered the bedroom and closed the door.

He wanted to be with Tess, to lather her body with soap and make love in the shower. But that wasn't going to happen with Bart and Soarez hovering in the other room. In the bathroom, he watched the outline of her body through the frosted glass of the shower. Her slender arms arched over her head as she rinsed her hair.

"I'm here," he said.

"Ready when you are."

"Oh, baby, I'm so ready." He was aching. "But Bart and Soarez are here. I've got to deal with them."

She glided the door to the shower open and peeked out. Her wet hair slicked back from her forehead. Droplets of water glistened on her skin. "Your loss," she teased.

He couldn't be this close and not touch her. He pulled her against his bare chest and kissed her hard. His hands slipped over her naked body. She was amazing—sexy and amazing.

"You're wet," she said.

"So are you."

"But I'm in a shower."

"Yeah." He didn't want to let her go. "I noticed."

"Take care of Bart. I'll join you in a minute."

He'd missed his chance for a shower with her. Though he knew there would be other times, he wanted to make love to her now, right now, damn it.

In the front room, Bart in his wheelchair sat at the table. Soarez was beside him. Nolan realized that his shirt was open. Usually, he tried to keep his scars hidden, but he didn't bother buttoning his shirt. Tess didn't find him repulsive, and her opinion was the only one that mattered.

He pulled out a chair and joined them. "What's up?"

"Victor isn't badly injured," Bart said. "It's only a flesh wound."

"Is he under arrest?"

"Not exactly."

Nolan leaned back in his chair and waited for the explanation. Bart was a wealthy and powerful man with connections at the highest level. He'd managed to skate around the rules and regulations when he arranged the death and burial of Joe Donovan. What had he set up for Victor?

"While I was with my son, I learned something about

myself," Bart said. "I wasn't a good dad. Victor was right about that. I wanted him to be strong and steady, and I refused to believe that he didn't meet my expectations."

"He's sick," Nolan said. "I'm guessing it's something like bipolar disorder."

"He needs treatment." Bart fixed him with a cool, blue-eyed gaze. "Victor was also right when he said that you were more like a son to me than he was."

His relationship with Bart was more intense than anything he'd shared with his own father before he died. "You're family to me—you and the rest of the CSaI guys."

"Now you have Tess and Joey."

"What's that about?" Soarez leaned forward. "She's your wife, right?"

"It's a long story, and I promise to give you all the details. But right now, I want to hear about Victor."

"He's in federal custody," Bart said.

"How did that happen?"

"Victor has valuable information about the weapons and drug trade in Iraq and Afghanistan. And he'll talk. I can't arrange to have the charges against him dismissed, but I've gotten clearance to transport him to a medical facility in Texas where he can get the treatment he needs."

Soarez checked his wristwatch. "We're leaving right now, taking a chopper from here to the hospital to pick up Victor and the marshal escorting him. Then we'll catch a private plane to Texas."

When Tess emerged from the bedroom, she was dressed in her casual clothes. With her wet hair tucked behind her ears and no makeup, she looked young and fresh. She hugged Bart and Soarez. They chatted about Lila and the Smithsonian and what she could expect to find in Freedom, Texas.

Nolan watched their interaction with rising apprehension. Something about this situation wasn't right. It wasn't just the way they avoided mentioning Nolan's real identity or Victor's threats that included holding a gun to Tess's head or the near murder of Pierre. Nolan didn't know what was bothering him.

After Bart and Soarez left for the helipad on the roof, Tess confronted him. "All right," she said. "What is it?"

"What's what?"

"You're tense, and I want to know why."

"I'm not sure." He crossed the room to the coffee table and poured himself another glass of wine. "I'm trying to put the pieces together. Something doesn't fit."

"Did you talk to Omar?"

He nodded slowly. "He told me to take care of Bart. I'm guessing that Bart's plans for his son have made some people mad."

"Like who?"

"He got Victor into federal custody which means he was talking to FBI, the marshal service and, of course, his CIA contacts. Not to mention tromping over jurisdictional issues with the local cops."

"Those are all people in law enforcement," she said. "They wouldn't actually hurt Bart. What about his enemies?"

Nolan clicked through the logic: Greenaway was at large. Bart, his enemy, was on his way to a helipad. One of the ground-to-air missile launchers was unaccounted for.

"I need to go to the roof."

She grasped his arm. "You're running headlong into danger again, aren't you?"

"Don't tell me to stop."

"I won't." She kissed his cheek. "Go save Bart. But come back to me."

NOLAN REACHED the hotel rooftop as the chopper was taking off. The helipad was well-lit but the rest of the roof was dark. The roar of the chopper blades blanked out every other sound. The air churned with hurricane force, and Nolan threw up a hand to shield his eyes.

Across the rooftop was a square structure that housed heating equipment. A dark figure separated from the shadows. He lifted a bazooka-like object—the missile launcher.

This wasn't an easy shot with a handgun, but all marines were trained marksmen. Nolan took aim and fired four shots. The man fell.

In seconds, Nolan had crossed the rooftop. He stood over the downed man, his gun aimed and ready to shoot again if necessary. One of his bullets must have nicked the carotid artery. Blood spurted from the wound.

"Joe Donovan." The man choked out his name. "You should be dead."

The voice registered in his memory. "Greenaway."

He gave a violent shudder. "I'll see you in hell."

"I've already been there and back."

Greenaway's eyes went blank. He was dead.

Finally, irrevocably, Nolan had his life back.

From this moment on, he was Joe Donovan.

Chapter Twenty-Three

By ten o'clock on Christmas morning in Freedom, Texas, Joey had already opened his presents and was outside playing with the border collie that belonged to the neighbors.

Tess stood watching him and enjoying the Texas sunshine. It felt good to be wearing only a light hoodie sweatshirt and jeans. She gazed up at her darling husband. They'd spent last night in bed together, and she was still feeling the afterglow.

"I could get used to this weather, Joe."

"It gets cold here, too. We have killer ice storms."

"This is a great place to live, especially for Joey. He'd have all this space to run around."

It went without saying that she and Joe would never live apart again, and she was trying to convince herself that she wouldn't be too upset if he wanted to stay here. He lived in a loft upstairs from the CSaI office. The space was spare and clean, furnished mostly with electronics, including a giant flat-screen television. If they had to live here, there would certainly be changes. "Your apartment needs work."

"I like our house in Arlington," Joe said. "That's home. That's where I want to raise our son."

Relieved, she grinned. "I'd like that. I could still have

my business. But does that really work for you? What about CSaI?"

"I could open a branch office in Washington. Everybody in that town needs security. We can figure it out." He leaned down and kissed her forehead. "Right now, I'm more concerned about our son."

Last night they'd told Joey that the man he knew as Nolan Law was really his father, Joe Donovan. Instead of questions, Joey said "okeydoke" and went to sleep. It was a difficult issue, and she wanted to handle it the right way.

She waved him over. Together, the three of them strolled toward the CSaI office and sat outside on the stoop. Tess took her son's little hand.

"Remember last night," she said. "I told you that Mr. Law was really Joe Donovan. We thought your daddy was dead, but he's not. He's here."

"And I love you very much," Joe said.

Joey's little forehead scrunched in a scowl. "Am I supposed to call you Mr. Law or Joe?"

"I know this is complicated," Tess said, "and you're going to have questions. You can ask us anything."

"I know what I can do." He turned toward Joe. "I'll call you Daddy."

Joe gave his son a loving hug. "Perfect."

AFTER LUNCH, they drove to Twin Harts, the sprawling ranch owned by Lila Lockhart. Tess wanted to drop in and apologize in person to the governor for the way her Christmas Eve event had turned out. The ranch house was gracious and beautiful; it reminded Tess of an antebellum mansion with pillars across the front.

Inside, Christmas decorations were everywhere— wreathes, bows, poinsettias, two trees and dozens of candles. Lila relaxed in the family room with her feet up on an ottoman. She wore only minimal makeup; it was clear that exhaustion had caught up with her. She'd rushed to the private jet to get back home for Christmas Day.

She waved. "Merry Christmas, y'all."

"Merry Christmas," Joey shouted. "This is my daddy. Can I go play with Zachary?"

"We're not staying long," Tess said. "You can say hello and come right back."

Joey looked to the left and the right. "I've never been here before. Where's Zachary's room?"

"He and his mom live in the guesthouse," Lila said. "But I think he's in the kitchen. Down that hallway."

Joey took off running, leaving them alone with the governor.

"Mr. Joe Donovan," Lila said, "you've got some explaining to do. It's nice to know I'm not the only one with secrets in my past."

"Not anymore," Joe said. "I'm with my family now. That's where I'll stay."

Before they got too far off track, Tess spoke up, "I wanted to tell you how sorry I was for not being present while your event was underway. That's not normally the way I do business."

"Everything was beautiful. The food was great. You did a brilliant job even while your life was being threatened. I'm recommending you to everybody I know in Washington."

The knot of tension in her chest loosened. "Thank you."

"I promise I won't be doing another big party on Christmas Eve. That time should be for families or for church."

Joe said, "Amen to that, Lila."

"Speaking of family, my whole gang was here for lunch, and we have good news. Bailey is pregnant."

"Congratulations," Tess said.

"It seems like every time I turn around I've got another grandchild." She covered her mouth as she yawned. "Oh my, excuse me. I should have taken more time to recuperate. All I want to do right now is sleep."

Stacy rushed into the room and greeted them. "I'm so glad Joey is here. Zachary keeps asking for him."

"They've become regular buddies, haven't they?" Tess was proud of Joey for the way he got along with Zachary. At times, Stacy's autistic son could be difficult.

"We were all heading out to the barn so Zachary could ride the horses," Stacy said. "Do you think Joey would want to come along?"

"Definitely," Tess said.

After saying goodbye to Lila, she walked with Stacy toward the barn. Joe had joined the other men from CSaI, Parker McKenna and Cody Wright. Joey and Zachary bounced along beside them, so excited that they couldn't hold themselves to a regular walk.

"How's the morning sickness?" Tess asked.

"Still there, but it's worth it."

"Thanks for last night," Tess said. "You handled the event really well."

"It wasn't me. Your plans were perfection. And Trudy is fantastic. Talk about calm under pressure, that woman deserves a medal."

An unbidden memory of Victor with Joe's Purple Heart popped into her mind. It was going to take a while to process everything that had happened. Lucky for her, she wouldn't have to go through it alone.

Stacy gestured to the boisterous group that was assembling near the horses. "These are the Lockharts. There's Bailey, Chloe and Devin. Grace is at the hospital with her son, Caleb."

Tess recalled that Caleb had a bone marrow transplant. Lila was the donor. "How is the boy doing?"

"Really well." Stacy pointed. "That handsome young man is Sean Lockhart. He's home on leave from Afghanistan."

In addition to Zachary and Joey, there were other kids: Devin's two-year-old baby and Parker's thirteen-year-old son, who lived with him and Bailey.

Tess and Stacy stood at the corral fence and watched as their little boys had a chance to be on horseback. Her gaze drifted toward Joe. Her big, strong husband was incredibly gentle with their son. The role of daddy suited him very well, indeed.

Even if they moved back to Arlington, she didn't want to lose touch with this place where Joe had lived. These people were his family, too.

THAT EVENING, Christmas dinner was at Bart's estate, and everybody was there—all the agents and their families, except for Grace Marshall and Nick Cavanaugh, who were with Caleb at the hospital.

They were all surprised by a commotion from outside the house. Bellowing *ho-ho-ho,* Santa Claus climbed down from a sleigh pulled by reindeer and marched through the front door carrying his goody bag over his shoulder.

Joe looked toward Bart. "When did you have time to arrange this?"

"It wasn't me," Bart said.

Santa set down his bag. A fancy script note pinned to the side said, *From Amelia.*

Joe had noticed her absence. "Where is she, anyway?"

Santa took out a letter and began to read. "Merry Christmas, I'm thinking of you while on vacation in Rio."

"Rio?" Joe said. "Rio de Janeiro?"

He was surprised, but not really. Amelia, the office manager and genius researcher, had a mysterious life that none of them were privy to.

Santa read from the letter, "Since all of you seem to be finding families, I think there should be a new name for Corps Security and Investigations."

Santa reached into a bag and pulled out one of a dozen teddy bears. It wore a T-shirt that said: Daddy Corps.

An appropriate name, Joe thought. No matter what else they did, they were daddies first.

Before they sat down to dinner, he had fielded half a dozen questions about who he really was. Joe called them all into one room. "Everybody find a seat. I'm going to explain this once and only once. Then, no more questions."

He was ready to step back into his life as Joe Donovan, and he needed them all to understand. He cleared his throat and launched into the story of how he nearly died and had to live undercover for five years until the threat to his wife and son was eliminated.

When he wrapped up the story, Bart wheeled himself toward him. The old man straightened his shoulders and saluted. In a gruff voice, he said, "Welcome home, Joe."

He held Tess in his arms and ruffled his son's hair. Joe Donovan truly was home. Exactly where he belonged.

* * * * *

SUSPENSE

Heartstopping stories of intrigue and mystery—
where true love always triumphs.

INTRIGUE

COMING NEXT MONTH
AVAILABLE JANUARY 10, 2012

#1323 CERTIFIED COWBOY
Bucking Bronc Lodge
Rita Herron

#1324 NATE
The Lawmen of Silver Creek Ranch
Delores Fossen

#1325 COWBOY CONSPIRACY
Sons of Troy Ledger
Joanna Wayne

#1326 GREEN BERET BODYGUARD
Brothers in Arms
Carol Ericson

#1327 SUDDEN INSIGHT
Mindbenders
Rebecca York

#1328 LAST SPY STANDING
Thriller
Dana Marton

You can find more information on upcoming Harlequin® titles,
free excerpts and more at www.HarlequinInsideRomance.com.

HICNM1211

REQUEST YOUR FREE BOOKS!
2 FREE NOVELS PLUS 2 FREE GIFTS!

Harlequin®

INTRIGUE®

BREATHTAKING ROMANTIC SUSPENSE

YES! Please send me 2 FREE Harlequin Intrigue® novels and my 2 FREE gifts (gifts are worth about $10). After receiving them, if I don't wish to receive any more books, I can return the shipping statement marked "cancel." If I don't cancel, I will receive 6 brand-new novels every month and be billed just $4.49 per book in the U.S. or $5.24 per book in Canada. That's a saving of at least 14% off the cover price! It's quite a bargain! Shipping and handling is just 50¢ per book in the U.S. and 75¢ per book in Canada.* I understand that accepting the 2 free books and gifts places me under no obligation to buy anything. I can always return a shipment and cancel at any time. Even if I never buy another book, the two free books and gifts are mine to keep forever.

182/382 HDN FEQ2

Name _____ (PLEASE PRINT) _____

Address _____ Apt. # _____

City _____ State/Prov. _____ Zip/Postal Code _____

Signature (if under 18, a parent or guardian must sign)

Mail to the **Reader Service:**
IN U.S.A.: P.O. Box 1867, Buffalo, NY 14240-1867
IN CANADA: P.O. Box 609, Fort Erie, Ontario L2A 5X3

Not valid for current subscribers to Harlequin Intrigue books.

**Are you a subscriber to Harlequin Intrigue books
and want to receive the larger-print edition?
Call 1-800-873-8635 or visit www.ReaderService.com.**

* Terms and prices subject to change without notice. Prices do not include applicable taxes. Sales tax applicable in N.Y. Canadian residents will be charged applicable taxes. Offer not valid in Quebec. This offer is limited to one order per household. All orders subject to credit approval. Credit or debit balances in a customer's account(s) may be offset by any other outstanding balance owed by or to the customer. Please allow 4 to 6 weeks for delivery. Offer available while quantities last.

Your Privacy—The Reader Service is committed to protecting your privacy. Our Privacy Policy is available online at www.ReaderService.com or upon request from the Reader Service.

We make a portion of our mailing list available to reputable third parties that offer products we believe may interest you. If you prefer that we not exchange your name with third parties, or if you wish to clarify or modify your communication preferences, please visit us at www.ReaderService.com/consumerschoice or write to us at Reader Service Preference Service, P.O. Box 9062, Buffalo, NY 14269. Include your complete name and address.

HI11B

*Brittany Grayson survived a horrible ordeal at the hands
of a serial killer known as The Professional...
who's after her now?*

*Harlequin® Romantic Suspense presents a new installment
in Carla Cassidy's reader-favorite miniseries,*
LAWMEN OF BLACK ROCK.

Enjoy a sneak peek of
TOOL BELT DEFENDER.

*Available January 2012
from Harlequin® Romantic Suspense.*

"**B**rittany?" His voice was deep and pleasant and made
her realize she'd been staring at him openmouthed through
the screen door.

"Yes, I'm Brittany and you must be…" Her mind suddenly went blank.

"Alex. Alex Crawford, Chad's friend. You called him
about a deck?"

As she unlocked the screen, she realized she wasn't
quite ready yet to allow a stranger inside, especially a male
stranger.

"Yes, I did. It's nice to meet you, Alex. Let's walk around
back and I'll show you what I have in mind," she said. She
frowned as she realized there was no car in her driveway.
"Did you walk here?" she asked.

His eyes were a warm blue that stood out against his
tanned face and was complemented by his slightly shaggy
dark hair. "I live three doors up." He pointed up the street to
the Walker home that had been on the market for a while.

"How long have you lived there?"

"I moved in about six weeks ago," he replied as they

walked around the side of the house.

That explained why she didn't know the Walkers had moved out and Mr. Hard Body had moved in. Six weeks ago she'd still been living at her brother Benjamin's house trying to heal from the trauma she'd lived through.

As they reached the backyard she motioned toward the broken brick patio just outside the back door. "What I'd like is a wooden deck big enough to hold a barbecue pit and an umbrella table and, of course, lots of people."

He nodded and pulled a tape measure from his tool belt. "An outdoor entertainment area," he said.

"Exactly," she replied and watched as he began to walk the site. The last thing Brittany had wanted to think about over the past eight months of her life was men. But looking at Alex Crawford definitely gave her a slight flutter of pure feminine pleasure.

Will Brittany be able to heal in the arms of Alex,
her hotter-than-sin handyman...or will a second
psychopath silence her forever? Find out in
TOOL BELT DEFENDER
Available January 2012
from Harlequin® Romantic Suspense
wherever books are sold.

♦ **Harlequin**®

SPECIAL EDITION

Life, Love and Family

Karen Templeton

introduces

The FORTUNES *of* TEXAS: Whirlwind Romance

When a tornado destroys Red Rock, Texas, Christina Hastings finds herself trapped in the rubble with telecommunications heir Scott Fortune. He's handsome, smart and everything Christina has learned to guard herself against. As they await rescue, an unlikely attraction forms between the two and Scott soon finds himself wanting to know about this mysterious beauty. But can he catch Christina before she runs away from her true feelings?

FORTUNE'S CINDERELLA

Available December 27th wherever books are sold!